"My lord, I find you difficult to understand."

Amethy's voice was puzzled. "Either you wished to have words with me or not."

"Not any precise ones," Northford muttered, irritation in his voice.

"If you had it in mind to speak to me about the incident in the caves today," Amethy went on, "or about the children on the lake—"

"That was not my intention." His tone turned cold; he removed his hand from her arm.

Amethy's temper flared. "Then, sir, will you express yourself so that I may know just what I've done?"

"Of all the henwitted females!" Northford exploded. "Did it never occur to you that a gentleman might care to spend some time in your company without argument, without the children—and without falling into a disaster!"

THE WINTER PICNIC

DIXIE McKEONE

Harlequin Books

TORONTO • NEW YORK • LONDON
AMSTERDAM • PARIS • SYDNEY • HAMBURG
STOCKHOLM • ATHENS • TOKYO • MILAN

Published March 1987
ISBN 0-373-31018-8

Printed in Canada

CHAPTER ONE

THE MOST NOBLE John William Carling Farringham, tenth Duke of Lowestroft, Earl of Coldfield, Viscount Alston, stuck out his bottom lip and stared balefully at the ancient stone wall of Lowestroft Castle, his ancestral estate. Before him, generations bearing his name and titles had looked upon that historic edifice with all the pride the famous castle deserved. They had been Farringhams of Lowestroft, and nothing could daunt the holders of that ancient and honoured position—they thought.

The present duke had none of those feelings. He was most certainly daunted, afraid, and stuck. Some thirty feet above the ground, he sat upon a thick limb of a massive oak tree, halfway between the huge trunk and the safety of the nursery window. His short sturdy legs encircled the limb, his small hands clasped firmly around a large branch above.

Noble children were usually called handsome, but Jackie, as his guardian called him, deserved the accolade. His looks were a legacy of the Farringhams, like his title and his considerable estates. His deep-auburn hair was straight but well cut and framed a porcelain complexion coloured by bright cheeks and deep brown eyes. The delicate eyebrows would thicken as he grew and would add weight to the sharpness of his aristocratic gaze, and he had already learned the trick of lowering with frightening suddenness. The infant roundness of his jaw and full lips would be chiselled by time to give evidence of an implacable nobleman whose blood carried in trust generations of pride in his family line. At the moment he was a handsome, sturdy and frightened little four-year-old boy.

He stared at the wall, or more correctly, one stone in the wall. His impressive property gave him no solace—it made him feel small and insignificant. The sudden fog had caused all but the nearest objects to fade to ghostly shapes that were unfamiliar and frightening.

Earlier that day he had climbed through the window to escape the nursery as he had heard his father used to do. At first he had felt very grown up to be out alone. Then while he was on an exploration of the lakeshore, searching for sea monsters or ducks, the mist rolled in and hid everything familiar in his world. If his father had suffered that experience, no one had ever mentioned it.

Finding his way back to the castle had been like one of his bad dreams, only worse, because Nurse Rae wasn't there to wake him and drive away the fears. When he finally arrived back at the tree, his new slippers were wet, he had fallen by the lake and dirtied his best green frock, and his white pantaloons with the green bows and pleated ruffles were dirty from climbing the tree.

And now he was stuck, his frock caught on a branch.

"Your Grace!" From below came the shocked tones of Tilbin, his butler. The little duke was dismayed at being caught, but nothing in his entire four years had prepared him for being trapped outside in the fog.

The dignity of a long line of dukes unconsciously rose in him. He searched his memory for the proper words to make his terrible situation seem commonplace.

"Tilbin, I very much fear I'm stuck," he said with what he hoped was a grown-up summary of his problem, but he couldn't quite stop the small sob that escaped him.

For a long moment Tilbin stared up at him, as frightening for Jackie as his predicament. Jackie had always been awed by the butler's dignity, which was considerably heightened by the stiff bearing of his portly frame and his leonine head of white hair.

After surveying the situation Tilbin looked around the fog-shrouded area, gave a resigned sigh and tested the strength of the lowest tree limb.

"Quite so," Tilbin replied with his usual unbending formality. "If you will be so good as to remain quite still—" Tilbin managed to climb onto the first limb "—quite still, your Grace, I will...oh dear...ah, I'm free. I will endeavour to come to your assistance."

As he ascended, Tilbin moved out of the child's sight, but from below came the sound of breaking twigs. To even think of his butler climbing a tree filled Jackie with awe. Then he realized there was no longer any noise below.

"Tilbin?" he called hesitantly. "Are you coming?"

"Uhmm—it does not appear so, your Grace. If you will give me a moment, I will try to extricate myself from a difficulty—I do plan on joining you shortly. It really *is* amazing just how many of these small branches—"

The butler was interrupted by the sudden opening of a casement window on the first floor. With a gasp the duke looked down to see the carefully disarranged dark curls of his cousin's head as he leaned forward for a better look.

"Good God!" exclaimed the Earl of Northford, the orphaned duke's guardian. "Tilbin, what the devil do you mean by climbing a tree? Are you in training for milling kens or some such?"

"Well—not precisely, my lord," the butler replied, with slightly less poise. "And I fear I'm not precisely climbing. The truth of the matter is, I find myself in some difficulty."

"Well you damned well should. And who were you talking to? Do you have help out there?"

The duke could not see the butler, but he knew Tilbin must have betrayed him, either by pointing or looking in his direction. The earl glanced up and started with surprise. For a moment he stared in amazement, but when he spoke his voice was calm.

"Don't move, Jackie," Northford ordered, speaking to the little duke. "Don't either of you move." With those instructions he disappeared back into the room.

"I really do not think I can move," Tilbin replied, his formal tones unimpaired by his predicament. "I trust, your Grace, that you are comfortably situated? If you will just keep your seat and hold to the branches we should shortly be rescued."

Jackie listened to Tilbin's encouragement without answering. Tears had blinded him for a moment, but he fought them off. It would be the worst thing in his world if his cousin should see him cry and consider him still a baby.

"My lord! Are you sure you wish to attempt this?" The butler sounded shocked and the duke looked down to see his cousin standing on the window ledge.

Jackie too was astonished. The earl stood barefoot, now wearing only his small clothes and snowy shirt, looking critically at the tree.

"Might as well," Northford said dispassionately. "I'd think it pretty tame to be the only sane one in the house."

After that statement he leapt forward, catching a limb and swinging like a monkey before he found a footing and moved out of sight. Jackie sat with an open mouth, staring down on the empty limbs onto which his grown-up and very elegant cousin had climbed with such expertise.

"Jackie, are you safe while I rescue Tilbin?" the earl called out.

"Yes, sir." Jackie answered, his voice full of relief. He was not afraid of falling. He had been frightened while he was lost in the fog, and being trapped in the tree.

Though he was unable to see what was happening in the lower part of the tree, he heard the snapping of several branches and his cousin spoke again.

"You're unsnagged, Tilbin. Just follow me—mind that branch—no, step where I step. Good God! Tilbin, you act as if you've never climbed a tree!"

"I regret to say, my lord, that it was not considered to be a necessary part of my training."

"You mean you never escaped from the nursery?"

"Hardly, my lord. Since I was not born to those advantages."

"Then we'll overlook the lack of skill, but just ask my young cousin. Having some monkey in the blood-line and a handy tree makes life easier. Right, Jackie?"

"Yes, sir." While the earl had been speaking, the duke could tell by the sound of his voice that he was drawing steadily closer. It was then no surprise to feel a reassuring pat on his shoulder. The snap of the branch that had caught the tail of his frock and held him prisoner told him he had been released, and Northford's firm grasp of his right arm made it easy for him to creep up the limb to the nursery window.

"You're in for it now," Northford said as he assisted Jackie over the windowsill and climbed in behind him.

"To bed after my dinner, and no story," Jackie prophesied, reciting the worst punishment he had yet endured. Nurse would probably scold, too.

"You had your adventure, now take your punishment like a man." The earl patted him on the shoulder again and turned back to the window to steady the butler as he crawled through the window.

Jackie turned and watched as Nurse Rae came hurrying into the room. He was too tired to heed much of his scolding, and after his adventure, being put to bed wasn't so bad after all.

Jackie awoke the next morning with mixed feelings. Both his anticipation and his dread were born of his dreams, he thought. He was dimly aware of having been frightened because of an argument between Northford and Nurse Rae over his tree. She was insisting the oak should be cut down, and Northford was saying the dukes of Lowestroft had been climbing out of that window for a hundred years and would continue to do so for another hundred.

Then he remembered that his cousin had planned to leave that morning on an inspection tour of his own estates and some of Jackie's outlying properties. Nurse might order the oak cut down in his absence. Jackie expected to hear the sounds of chopping at any moment! He jumped from his bed and raced to the window.

"My tree! They can't cut it down!" he cried, searching for evidence of the gardeners approaching with axes.

"Come back, young man, and put on your slippers," Nurse Rae called. "You needn't bother to look—it's still there, though the Lord only knows why he should not have it chopped down to the ground."

"My cousin knows I like it, that's why." Jackie hurried back to where she held out his felt slippers, obeying not out of blind obedience, but because of the cold floor.

"That wasn't the Lord I was speaking of," she replied as she helped him into his morning robe and led him over to the small table by the fire. His porridge was steaming until she stirred in the correct portion of milk to make it nicely warm. While he occupied himself with the bowl and spoon, she completed the toasting of his bread and brought it hot from the fire.

As she approached the table he looked up from his breakfast, fingering the edge of the table. "Then you did argue with Northford? I wasn't dreaming?"

"You were supposed to be sleeping," she admonished him. "It isn't proper or mannerly to listen in on other people's conversations."

"I didn't know I was listening," he replied, idly stirring his porridge. Suddenly he recalled the exciting part of what he had thought a dream. Northford had said Jackie climbed out of the window because his life was too restricted for a child his age. His cousin's reasoning meant nothing to Jackie, but he liked Northford's solution, which was for him to have playmates. He looked up hopefully. "Then I am to go to Halstead Manor and play with the boys there? Or was that part a dream?" He gazed up hopefully.

"No, you shall go, unless I find you've climbed through the window again. I warn you, your Grace, behave or I won't take you."

Three interminable days passed during which time notes were sent back and forth between Lowestroft Castle and Halstead Manor, seven miles distant. Then a groom brought the much-awaited missive that threw Jackie into high glee. He could hardly wait for the next day when he and Nurse would go on the visit.

Doubts assailed him in the carriage on the way, but when he arrived he was delighted to find that the Viscount something, who was Edward, and the Honourable Willy were very good fellows. Even though Edward was two years older he was no larger than Jackie, and Willy, who was also four, was a little smaller than Jackie. They were the best of friends in an hour and played in the garden all afternoon.

The pleasure of making new friends was not the most memorable experience to be impressed upon Jackie that afternoon. When Willy fell and scraped his hand, his wails brought Lady Halstead into the garden and Jackie discovered the meaning of "mother."

Jackie was barely six months old when both his parents were carried off by an epidemic. He knew the words "parents," "mother" and "father," but they had no real meaning for him and he had never felt a lack in his life. His wonderful cousin was a substitute for his father, and female affection was supplied by his nurse. Not until Lady Halstead took Willy on her lap and soothed him, did Jackie know there was a special relationship between mothers and their children. He was suddenly aware of what he was missing.

So it was not surprising that in this sudden knowledge of his lack, he was struck by the entrance on the scene of Miss Amethy Portney. His experience was not great, but one look told him the young lady who walked across the garden was as lovely as the fairy princesses in his books.

When he asked Edward about her, his new friend told him she was his cousin, and his mother was worried about her because she wasn't married. His mother hoped she might introduce Cousin Amethy to an eligible man with whom she would fall in love. Edward didn't quite understand what eligible was, but she might meet a man who had it.

Jackie didn't know what it was, either, but he knew all about marriage. In his storybooks the handsome princes married the beautiful princesses and they lived happily ever after.

Mothers and fathers were married.

An idea, as yet so vague it had no words, was growing in his mind.

Jackie made the acquaintance of Miss Amethy when she presided over the blue-and-white teapot in the nursery. So much milk was added to his cup that the tea hardly warmed it, but he was too intent on drinking it to object. Three times he emptied his cup so he could go back and stand close to Miss Amethy when she refilled it. He was upset when Nurse Rae insisted he should have no more, but Miss Amethy had understood and had allowed him to sit by her and hand out the little cakes on small plates.

When they left Halstead Manor and were on their way back to Lowestroft, he sat quietly in the landau, thinking about Miss Amethy. She was as beautiful as a princess. Would a prince come and take her away? Though he wasn't a prince, Cousin Northford was the most wonderful man Jackie knew.

Jackie wanted a mother.

The idea was becoming a wish; he thought about what Edward said and an idea was taking hazy form....

If Northford and Miss Amethy were to marry...

Nurse Rae misuhderstood his silence, and assuming him to be overtired, she wrapped a robe about him, drawing him close to her bony side. At any other time he would have objected to being treated as if he were still an infant, but at the moment he was too occupied to demur.

He thought until the carriage halted in front of the tall stone arch framing the entrance of the castle. When Nurse Rae picked up the large straw bag she carried with her on visits, he pushed himself back against the seat.

"I'll help Perkins stable the horses," he announced. The head groom and part-time coachman was Jackie's special friend. Perkins's indomitable spirit and laughing green eyes showed his half-Irish blood, and the tall lanky man knew how to play to a nicety the multiple roles of friend, confidant, mentor and servant to the noble orphan.

"I think Perkins can manage," Nurse Rae replied, smoothing his hair. "You should be taking your bath."

"But I'm not all dirty anymore!" Jackie objected angrily. "You washed my face and hands before tea, and I haven't done anything dirty since." His newly discovered dignity was fast deserting him. Nurse Rae saw him blinking and took out her handkerchief, but he shook his head. He was determined not to let the groom see him cry.

Nurse Rae shook her head and sighed in defeat. "He's overtired, Perkins, so he mustn't stay long. Letting him go is better than a temper fit, I suppose. Mind you see he keeps away from the horses now."

When the nurse had entered the castle, Jackie rode in solitary state around the drive to the carriage house, sitting quietly until the landau had been pulled up to the wide doors of the carriage house and the building sheltered them from any view within the castle.

"Mind you keep those beasts away from his Grace!" Perkins roared at the stableboys who had begun to unhitch the horses.

"Make way for his Grace!" Perkins shouted again for the benefit of any listening ears. Meanwhile he was engaged in lifting Jackie onto the back of Cloudy, the big grey left-wheeler, and the placid mare lumbered slowly into the stable.

"Won't we have to walk them around and cool them off?" Jackie asked, disappointed that they were heading straight for the stalls.

"Not after driving Nurse Rae, we won't," Perkins said, laughing. "If we was to break into a trot, she'd swear I was out to kill the pair of you—uh—" Perkins looked disconcerted. "What I mean is, she likes to ride slow and look at the scenery."

The duke was not to be fobbed off with an explanation that wouldn't fool a baby. "You mean Nurse is not an out-and-outer like Northford," he observed.

Perkins looked shocked. "Now see here, your Grace, where did you pick up that cant?"

Small as he was, Jackie had learned the value of friends who protected their cronies by overlooking small indiscretions. He had no intention of admitting who the tutor of colourful expressions might be, though Holmes, the undergroom, threw him a scared look.

"Mustn't I say it?" Jackie asked innocently.

"It ain't for the likes of you to be repeating what you hear in the stables, mind."

"Oh." Jackie waited until Holmes had removed and carried away the trappings from Cloudy's stall. When Perkins picked up a brush to groom the shoulders of the horse, Jackie crawled onto the croup and sat watching. For once he was not totally absorbed in the activities of the stables. His idea was taking shape. He carefully formed his speech in his mind, just as Northford had said the words to him.

"Perkins," he said slowly, hoping he sounded important. "I think we should have a talk, just between gentlemen."

"If you say so, your Grace," Perkins answered, and Jackie wondered if the groom had grinned just before he ducked his head.

"Perkins," he said more firmly. "You just got married. How do you like being married?"

The groom had been bending over, brushing Cloudy's foreleg, but he straightened quickly, his face a study in surprise. Across the stable, one of the undergrooms gave a laugh, quickly cut off by the head groom's glare. Perkins gulped and sighed deeply before answering.

"Well, your Grace, it's the natural thing to do, and a fine thing it is, but I'm thinking that your Grace might be a few years too young to be bothering his head with it."

Jackie nodded at the groom's wisdom. The only married people he knew were quite old and grown-up.

"But Northford's not too young. It would be very nice if he were to marry."

"There's many as is thinking the same thing," mumbled Perkins before he recollected to whom he spoke. He looked up, startled.

"See here, your Grace," he said loudly. "It ain't for either of us to make that decision—you see, son—your Grace, that's kind of a personal thing—" He was interrupted by two stableboys in a stall close by.

"Ain't likely you'll be gettin' his lordship within shouting distance of an eligible female," one said, laughing.

"He says they're more dangerous than killer horses," the other replied.

Perkins turned red in the face. He stood, one hand on Cloudy, obviously debating the danger of leaving the little duke alone on the horse versus the harm the stableboys could do with their unchecked tongues. As was his duty, he stayed by his post, but his shout rang in the rafters.

"Keep your tongues in your heads, or I'll have the skin off your backs!" he roared.

Jackie was dismayed by the remarks of the stable-boys. He had a profound respect for their knowledge-able attitudes and their colourful language. He was of the opinion that they must know everything. To learn that the earl had a predilection against marriageable females was a severe blow to his hopes.

"But, Miss Amethy isn't dangerous," he insisted, growing angry at himself as well as the others when his voice rose in a wail. He mastered his tone a bit, but he still sounded petulant when he announced, "And Miss Amethy is very beautiful!"

In the rare times Jackie was allowed in the stables, he was usually only coaxed back to the nursery after considerable effort, but he was disappointed and de-cided to retire to think over his problem. He had an active mind and an optimistic nature. By the time Perkins had taken him to the castle and left him in charge of a footman, Jackie had formed a plan. They were crossing the inner courtyard when the duke stopped and looked up at the liveried servant.

"I wish to see Tilbin," he said, freeing his hand from the larger one.

A cautious look from the footman told him he would meet with no formidable resistance. Some of his servants ordered him about, and weren't afraid to pick him up and forcibly move him if he resisted, but oth-ers were less likely to interfere. He had yet to under-stand it, but he knew when to put it to his use. He puffed himself up with a deep breath.

"*I* will take the responsibility," he announced, again aping his cousin. While the footman was trying to think of a suitable answer, Jackie marched away and entered the butler's pantry, confronting a sur-prised Tilbin.

"I want to have a party for my new friends, Tilbin," he informed the butler while the mood of hauteur was still inflating him. "A luncheon. I want Northford to come. Please, when will he be back?"

He waited anxiously while the butler looked down at him as if struck dumb. Jackie was wondering if he had done it properly, because when Northford said such things Tilbin usually bowed and said, "Very good, my lord." The air Jackie had forced into his lungs made his ribs hurt, but if he didn't keep his chest out and his chin up, he might cry. He was relieved when the butler finally answered him.

"It's hard to say when the earl will return, your Grace. If it meets with Nurse Rae's approval, I see no reason why a luncheon in the nursery could not be arranged. Should I discuss the matter with her?"

Jackie was dismayed. "No! I do not wish a nursery party! Miss Amethy would not meet Northford, because he never comes to lunch up there!"

Tilbin looked at him in wonder. "Miss Amethy, I gather, is your new friend?"

"Yes, and I want her to meet my cousin. She is the most beautiful lady, and much too big for nursery chairs."

"Too big for—oh, my." Tilbin eyed the duke with acute discomfort until a sudden look of relief transformed his face. "Your Grace, I do believe I hear Nurse Rae asking for you. If you will just step up to the nursery, I'll see what we can do about your party. I do think you had better go—Nurse will be overset if she's unable to locate you."

Jackie allowed himself to be hurried up to the nursery by the footman, but he knew the butler had given him a Banbury Tale. None of his ideas were going to get the beautiful Miss Amethy and his cousin to meet and fall in love.

He submitted to his bath and to being dressed in his nightclothes without protest. Nurse Rae, seeing his downcast face, drew him on to her lap while she combed his hair.

"I think my little gentleman is very tired tonight. You had such a busy day."

His tears, for the past hour just under the surface of his emotions, were brought out by her sympathy.

"But it didn't go right at all," he said, sniffling.

"I thought you had a good time, and you certainly laughed a lot when you played in the garden," she said as she cuddled him close, rocking him.

"But Holmes said Northford didn't like pretty ladies who got married, and Tilbin wouldn't say I could have a luncheon party—" he explained, sobbing, all his frustrations coming out at one time. "Now I will never get my cousin to see how pretty Miss Amethy is and make her my mother."

When Nurse Rae stopped rocking and looked down at him in surprise, he mistook her feelings. He threw his arms around her neck, clutching her close. "Oh, I love you, Nurse, but Willy and Edward have a nurse and a mother. Why can't I have a mother?"

She gathered him close, but not before he saw the tears in her eyes. "Oh, my poor little man! I can't answer that, my sweet, but you shall have some bread and milk and go to sleep. Things will look better in the morning."

Things looked worse in the night. The duke awoke to face the disappearing monster from his nightmare. Usually Nurse Rae would come in, the tail of her nightgown flapping, and angrily order away all the bad things that came in dreams, but though her door was open, he didn't hear her. Taking his courage in one hand, he brandished his only weapon, his pillow, in the other.

"Get out of here, you—thing!" he shouted, unsure what the apparition had been. Satisfied that he had banished his foe, he sat and waited for Nurse Rae to tuck him up again. After a few minutes he decided he must remind her of her duty, but when he went to her door she was neither in the bed nor in the room. At first he stood frowning, unable to believe she wasn't where she was expected to be. Her absence was an outrage against his sense of fitness. Though he might escape to seek adventure, it was not at all the thing for Nurse to do so.

It was a considerable undertaking to start wandering through the castle at night, but at that moment it seemed preferable to going to sleep alone. He put on his slippers, took his candle and went into the hall, pausing in the doorway while he wondered where the banished monsters of his dreams went. Not into the halls, he decided. If they ran from him and Nurse, they certainly wouldn't risk facing Tilbin.

In the darkness, the stairs and halls seemed to go on forever, but he finally approached the open door of the Room. He had planned to march right in, but what he overheard stopped him.

"And of course he wants a mother!" Nurse Rae was saying. "Mind you, it would be a good thing for Lord Northford to marry, too. It would likely stop his gallivanting all over the country."

"You can't call his present journey gallivanting," Tilbin protested. "He is at present taking an inspection tour of several outlying properties."

"That's all good and well," Perkins replied, "but you tell me how you're going to get his lordship to go traipsing after this young female. Lord, he'll get one whiff of a marriageable chit's perfume and not go within a mile of her. Lightskirts, that's all he bothers with. Here today, forgotten tomorrow. That's his way."

"I think we might effect a meeting," Tilbin announced with authority. "Though it is a shame Nurse Rae is so healthy."

"And a lot of good I would be to the child if I were forever down with the vapours or a migraine."

"On the contrary," Tilbin countered. "If, after the earl returns, his Grace was anticipating a visit to Halstead Manor—you had a migraine, and the maids were either off or entirely too busy to escort his Grace, I'm sure the earl would do so. For all his rakish ways, my lord is uncommonly concerned for his Grace's happiness."

"It might work," Perkins said thoughtfully. "Personally I like the little fellow's idea. Have a party."

"Perkins," Tilbin said frostily, "a child of four may not host an adult party. It would be quite outside the limits of propriety to have children at an adult gathering."

"Not if it was a picnic," the groom argued.

"Well, I won't have that," Nurse Rae retorted. "I'll not have my little gentleman sitting on the damp ground, and neither would the Halstead woman, for all her flighty ways."

"Woman, don't be hen-witted!" Perkins roared in his stable voice. "I lent most of my men to bring the potted plants and the garden furniture into the old ballroom for the winter. Why couldn't you arrange them and put some leaves and rushes on the floor—maybe some sand? What's wrong with a picnic inside? Then just tell Lady Susan you did it just as she ordered. She's so absentminded, she'll never know the difference."

"Perkins!" Tilbin's voice was enthusiastic. "I do think it would do! We could describe it as a winter picnic. Just the thing, and his Grace's great-aunt Lady Susan will be delighted she thought of it."

The duke almost squealed with excitement before he stopped himself and hurried up the steps. In his room again, he put his candle on the table and kicked off his slippers. He had climbed into bed before he remembered he wanted someone to tuck him up. Soon, he decided, he would have a mother to do that. A beautiful mother who laughed and gave him tea and sugar biscuits.

CHAPTER TWO

THE HONOURABLE Miss Amethyst Carolyn Portney was dressed in a morning gown of pale blue, and in the latest fashion, since she had not long come into the country after her third short season in London. Her golden blond and waywardly curling hair was rather sketchily confined by a blue ribbon that matched the dress and was her only concession to her appearance. It was most fortunate, therefore, that her locks were at their most charming in a disarray that would reduce most females to deplorable conditions. The wispy blond curls that warred obstinately against maids, dressers and hot curling irons only desired to be left to themselves, so they could frame her face in tiny gold circlets and crown the top of her head in soft waves. It was not vanity that caused Amethy to allow them to go their own way, but a total disregard. She too often had other things to occupy her mind.

At the moment, she was concerned with a button.

Her deep blue-violet eyes that had occasioned her name were lowered to her work and covered by lids generously fringed in dark long lashes. Her mouth, a naturally pink bow, was slightly pursed as she concentrated on her work, but the fetching picture of herself and her industry was totally lost on Viscount Slathon. Edward's six-year-old mind was somewhat anxiously occupied by the fact that his jacket was still in his cousin's lap.

He bounded up and down on one impatient foot, his entreaties for haste a bit impeded by his wayward tongue that kept protruding into the gap caused by the loss of his two front teeth. He impatiently brushed back a lock of dark blond hair and wrinkled a freckled nose.

"Oh, hurry, Amethy, do pleathe," he lisped. "Jackie will thoon be here and he doethn't care if I have a hole in my coat."

Amethy looked up and smiled at the anxious child. "Only a moment, Edward, and it will be ready for you to tear again, which you certainly must do if you play as hard as you did the last time his Grace visited."

At that moment Willy, Edward's four-year-old brother, dashed into the room, his eyes shining with tears. His was a complexion that deepened with distress, and at the moment his face was nearly as red as his hair. His freckles, a feature he shared with his brother, were for the moment nearly hidden by his flush. With a total disregard for his cousin's present activity, he threw himself into her arms.

"Someone's coming on a horse!" he wailed. "Please, Amethy, don't let it be a groom from Lowestroft saying Grace Jackie can't come."

"Oh, I hope it will not be the groom from Lowestroft, I must be so disappointed. You'll have to help me have a happy day, else I will wish to cry, too." Amethy stopped her sewing long enough to wipe away Willy's tears. No others were forthcoming because her mention of her own disappointment had so astonished him that he stood staring for a moment.

Then, with the awkwardness of a newly born gallantry, he climbed into the chair beside her, crushing
her skirt and knocking off the button box while he
patted her arm consolingly.

Despite Willy's well-intentioned hindrance, she soon
finished the repair of Edward's coat and helped him
into it. Then she inspected both the boys critically, assuring herself that no fault could be found with their
appearance.

She had promised Nurse Kerns to keep the children
presentable. Thinking of the worthy woman who was
in a flurry above stairs made her smile. The Halstead
nurse was determined that Nurse Rae would find
nothing in the Halstead nursery at which she could lift
her already somewhat lofty nose. The other might
serve a duke but Elsa Kerns intended to prove that her
little noblemen were wanting for nothing. If any employer, she indicated when Lady Halstead objected, so
forgot themselves as to think their wishes came before the task of impressing a duke's nurse, Nurse
Kerns was more than ready to apprise them of their
error.

Amethy had cheerfully volunteered to look after the
boys. Since the prospect of losing the Nurse because
of a new charge soon due in the cradle had thrown
Lady·Halstead into a lively fear for the future, Amethy was able to send her aunt away, assuring her she
would enjoy the company of the children. Indeed she
did. They spent pleasant evenings while she read them
her favourite stories of King Arthur, Sir Lancelot and
Sir Galahad. She often made up stories of knights and
dragons that kept them wide-eyed.

Amethy felt at home and at peace with the Hal-
steads and the boys. Occasionally she gave a wistful

sigh that she might not remain at Halstead Manor or at least return to Five Oaks, her father's home near Dover. She knew her wish to remain permanently at either place was futile.

Her loving but retiring father had set his heart upon a good marriage for her and was determined she should have it. He had never ceased to grieve for Amethy's mother, who died when Amethy was twelve, and felt he could do no more for his daughter than to see that she found the happiness he had shared with his beloved.

Even though he was fond of Lady Halstead, his youngest sister, Amethy was hard pressed to get his blessing for her visit to Halstead Manor. He could not imagine her meeting anyone of consequence in rural Derbyshire.

He much preferred Amethy to remain in society with his older sister, Lady Grimwald. He was sure only the circumstance of Amethy's being in the right place at the proper time would answer his purpose for her.

Amethy knew why she had not succeeded in fulfilling her parent's expectations, though she had been in society for three years. The past several seasons had been graced by young ladies with not only beauty but extremely large dowries, something with which Amethy was not blessed, and a fact she refused to point out to her doting parent. Their name was a very old and proud one, but her father had been, since she could remember, struggling valiantly to restore the fortunes wasted by his own father. To enlarge her dowry would render him almost penniless and only serve to purchase what she refused to buy.

To Amethy, those gentlemen who gave weight to monetary considerations when looking for a wife were lacking in nobility of character. Lady Grimwald, who fully understood the necessities of the social set, accused Amethy of living in a storybook world, but Amethy had her own standards and was not ready to settle for less.

In justice to the young lady, her father had received no less than four offers for her hand, but he was not overly pleased with two of them, and since his daughter's heart had not been engaged, she was allowed to refuse.

Amethy knew, too, that a part of the difficulty was her utter boredom with "polite" society. An hour of foolish commonplaces sent her mind wandering off into a world of its own, at times making people think she was insipid. Long involved discussions on the virtues of a bit of Spanish mixture added to a blend of snuff was enough to make her wish she was a vaporous female. She much preferred the company of Willy, Edward and her aunt if she could not be at home with her father. She missed their shared enjoyment of a classic poem, a game of chess and visiting their tenants.

She was drawn out of her thoughts as Willy tugged gently at her sleeve.

"I'll play with you if you like," Willy said shyly. "So if Grace Jackie cannot come, you mustn't be sad."

"If he doesn't arrive, I'll tell you what we must do," she answered brightly. "We'll finish making the paper farm. We have ducks and sheep, but I think there are ever so many animals we could make...."

Just then the door to the small sitting room was thrown open and Amethy's aunt, Lady Halstead, bustled into the room, her pretty round face a study in alarm. Her lace cap was askew and a blond curl, a legacy of her Portney blood, bounced against her cheek. Her small, plump figure showed that a family increase was shortly expected.

"Lord, Amethy! It's him!"

To that dramatic but somewhat ambiguous statement, her niece looked up blankly, questioning her aunt in an equally ungrammatical manner.

"Him who?"

"Him!" Lady Halstead threw out her hand wildly, her dark blue eyes rolling to the ceiling. "The Earl of Northford! Desmond Marling! He's here!"

Her aunt's dismay was understandable. Had she said the angel Lucifer was paying a visit, Lady Halstead would have had no more reason to be alarmed. Desmond Marling was a name Amethy had never heard. But Northford, as he was universally known, was usually spoken of in whispers within society in London, and tales of him were most often accompanied by titillated laughter. His exploits were avidly repeated behind fluttering fans, and little sighs were not unusual when he was mentioned.

The "polite" world was never bothered by him during the Season. He was reputed to be a disastrously charming rake, so it was Amethy's opinion that the matrons' sighs contained relief. He could be ruinous to any female's reputation, it was said.

His history, as told to her, was indeed a colourful one. Northford was rumoured to have fought a duel at nineteen in which he killed his man and fled to France at the insistence of his family. There he was reputed to have taken an Austrian countess from her husband and moved on to Italy.

For five years, tales of his amorous adventures were brought back from France. Then he returned to England with an Italian singer. For two years he had brazenly hosted the extravagant parties given by his vivacious lightskirt, but the arrival of another Austrian beauty ousted the Latin in his affection. That attachment was said to have been of short duration.

The charms of the Corinthian spirit at that time invading the gentlemen of society had won him over, so his romantic adventures were interspersed with tales of his physical prowess and of his ability to outdrive every gentleman in London. Then, in Amethy's second season, questions were mingled with the gossip. He was not very much in evidence anywhere.

For her part, Amethy was not disappointed by the absence of a villain who must delight in destroying the comfort of others. The type of female who would be attracted by such a person was, to Amethy, lacking in decency.

"Quite odious of Thomas to go off with his bailiff today," Lady Halstead was saying as she caught sight of herself in the mirror and hastened to tuck away her curls and straighten her cap. "I asked him not to go out, since the weather is threatening, and now here I am, having to entertain that man! Amethy, you must come down! I will not be alone with him."

"Don't ask me," Amethy said weakly. "I have no wish to meet him."

"Neither have I!" her aunt retorted. "But you must come, dearest. I cannot be alone with him. Come quickly, boys."

Amethy wondered why the children would be required, but her aunt departed in an agitated flutter, Amethy's questions unanswered. They had just seated themselves in the drawing room when the butler announced the Duke of Lowestroft and the Earl of Northford.

After the years of gossip, it was somewhat shocking for Amethy to see the famous rake, who entered holding the hand of the four-year-old child.

She was both disappointed and intrigued by the man who crossed the drawing room. Lord Byron's influence had left a trail of imitators who affected both a studied casualness in their attire and an air of brooding mystery that hinted at dark deeds in their past. The one man who could claim more right to that demeanour than even the famous fictional character of the noted poet affected none of those attributes.

Northford was tall and well built, as his reputation as a Corinthian suggested. His hair immediately caught Amethy's attention; it lacked the heavy pomading normally used by gentlemen of fashion though its dusky black waves naturally fell into a reasonable facsimile of the cherubim. His somewhat narrow face would have been overshadowed by his high-bridged nose but its effect was softened by large deep-grey, questing eyes that seemed to search out and record every detail of the room at a glance.

Eyes that saw freshly. Amethy, not at all poetic despite her love of the old stories, was surprised at the thought that entered her head.

Contrary to fashion, he was deeply tanned. His dress befitted a country gentleman, blue superfine bathcloth coat, buckskins and top boots. The cut of his clothing descried the best of London tailors, but the white tops on his boots were only of moderate cut.

He entered the room with a poise akin to arrogance, but Amethy thought she detected a certain wariness in his eye. The leg he made his hostess was graceful and lacked no effort. His voice was cool, his apology one of manners rather than sincerity.

"Forgive the sudden intrusion, Lady Halstead, but I have been temporarily elevated to the position of nurse. I understand a schoolroom party takes precedence over even a royal command, and that Nurse Kerns will instruct me in my duties."

"Well—oh—well—my heavens!" Lady Halstead threw both hands to her mouth at the thought of the earl in the schoolroom. She stared with anxious eyes at the tall handsome man who watched her with some amusement. While she attempted to puzzle out the dilemma, her sons' enthusiasm overcame their training and they bounded across the room, converging on their new friend.

"We thought you might not come," Willy announced in a voice pitched high with excitement.

Jackie, who had been standing quietly by Northford, turned to face them. "I rode on Cousin Northford's horse!" he shrilled. "All the way from Lowestroft!"

Young Edward could not be left out of the conversation. "Amethy ith going to make a paper farm that thtandth up and everything!" he volunteered, trying to lead Jackie away from their elders, but by the simple expedient of catching his ward by the collar, the earl detained his small relative.

"Rein in," Northford commanded. "Let's have a leg for your hostess."

Jackie, mindful of his instructions, turned back to make his bow. He was in such haste that his training deserted him, and he would have been completely overset had his cousin not caught him just in time to keep him from falling on his face. Then Northford turned his ward around bodily and gently shoved him in the direction of his playfellows.

The earl, seeing that his hostess's agitation was turning from his sudden arrival and was about to centre itself on the lack of decorum in her sons, forestalled her.

"I trust we will have succeeded in making them human before we must thrust them on society, but for my part, I dislike holding my little beast on too tight a leash."

The children had converged upon Amethy, talking in happy little shrieks, and beyond them, Lady Halstead and the earl were also approaching the couch on which she sat.

Her aunt was busy explaining to the earl that Amethy was visiting her after being in London for the short season, whereupon the expressions flitting across Northford's face brought up every sense of outrage in Amethy. As clearly as if the words were printed on his face, she saw his reaction. He had been cozened into coming to Halstead Manor to meet an eligible female. The slight look of boredom indicated he would endure it, the resignation was a quite obvious comment on the number of times he had endured similar situations.

Amethy had protested against meeting the man and found the situation intolerable. His expression had shown him to have as much gallantry as she'd expect from a robber or a court jester. Her greeting was therefore most perfunctory, and the lack of pleasure in her greeting was apparent, almost rag-mannered.

Far from being discomfited by her coolness, Northford seemed at first surprised and then amused by it. "Ah, too late I see. Jackie is before me and has captured the heart of the lady."

"I'm sure no lady was ever more fortunate," she replied primly, withdrawing her hand from his a bit too quickly for the proprieties.

The earl cocked an eyebrow and gave a smile, partly inquisitive, yet with a sardonic tinge that gave him a Lucifer-like appearance. He seemed about to make an answer, but the four-year-old Willy had more important matters to discuss.

"May we make the paper farm now, Amethy?" he broke in, tugging at her skirt. "I think Jackie would like it very much."

"Would I?" The little duke's eyes widened as he looked from Willy to Amethy.

"I hope so. Let's go to the nursery, and we'll see." Amethy made her voice unnaturally bright as she spoke to the children. Her aunt would be upset to be left alone with the earl, but Amethy judged it better to leave than give out with the set-down she felt building within her. She was leading the children across the room when she was stopped by Jackie, who held her left hand, and caught that of the earl with his other.

"Have you ever seen a paper farm, sir?" Jackie asked.

"No, and I'm enthralled at the thought of adding to my knowledge." The earl started walking towards the door with Amethy and the boys. When she hesitated, staring at him in dismay, his smile became almost satanic. "I wouldn't miss it for the world. And you know, I am instructed to go to the nursery."

"Oh no, sir!" Lady Halstead quaked, clasping her hands together. "I am convinced you could not be comfortable. The chairs are so small. If a paper farm it must be, then I think it should be made here. The nurse would not like us to invade the playroom with too much clutter.''

At that time a footman entered with a tray of refreshments, and the boys abandoned Amethy to accept glasses of lemonade and to explore the delicate silver epergne with hanging baskets containing macaroons and candied fruits. For the ladies there was ratafia and a port for Lord Northford. By the time the lemonade had disappeared and the epergne's baskets had been emptied, the footman had returned carrying a brown paper parcel.

When the string had been removed, the package opened to reveal more than a score of folded sheets of the same brown wrapping. Lying on top of the stack were several unlikely scraps gleefully pounced upon by the two Halstead boys. While Jackie watched in fascination, they folded the scraps along already creased lines to shape ducks and sheep. And if some of the paper animals were a bit tilted here and there, and two had to lean against others to remain upright at all, it obviously went unnoticed by their small owners.

Willy and Jackie were at once occupied in placing the ducks upon the scalloped centre pattern of the Savonnerie carpet. Then with a concerned eye at the clouds seen through the window, Edward began to take them away from the younger boys, gathering them in a small huddle. Jackie, too well-mannered to complain, sadly watched the removal of the toys, but Willy's brow darkened and he was ready to draw his brother's cork in high fashion. Edward's complaint forestalled him.

''Amethy, our theep need a houthe, or the rain will get them wet,'' he complained.

Willy had a better idea. "We must have a barn—just like the big one behind the stables," he cried.

Amethy, who was known for her talent at tearing paper into the most intricate and lifelike shapes of animals, looked at the boys in surprise. She was about to say it was beyond her power to create a building, and they must be satisfied to shelter their animals under the sofa, but the mocking look of the earl caused her to bite back her words. He had taken a chair that he had turned to face the couch to converse with Lady Halstead while he watched the creation of two pigs. But when Amethy showed her puzzlement at the idea of constructing a barn, he smiled. The right corner of his mouth turned up in what Amethy chose to regard as a smirk.

Amethy threw him a venomous look and bit her lip. To be truly just to the talented young lady, she made every effort to ascertain how the wrapping paper, so malleable when she wanted to create an animal, could be forced into a shape even similar to a barn, but her lack of truly mechanical ideas extended even to this small matter. She made an exasperated sound and threw the paper down in disgust. When she raised her eyes, the earl's smile had widened, causing her to lose control over her tongue.

"I fail to think the matter humourous, sir, and I suggest if you can do better, you are welcome to try!" Amethy bit her lower lip, ashamed of being rude. She was about to apologize when the earl rose and abruptly left the room.

"Oh, my dear." Lady Halstead lowered the embroidery on which she was adding a stitch from time to time. "I don't know but what you had cause, but should you..." Her words faded away, her concern no more evident than her confusion.

"I'm sorry, Aunt Mary, but I just..." Amethy stifled the rest as the sound of quick footsteps echoed in the hall and the earl reentered the drawing room and crossed to where Amethy and the boys were surrounded by the brown paper and animals. Jackie looked up, alarmed.

"It isn't time to go?" he asked Northford, in a small voice.

"No, brat, I was taking a look at the barn." Northford pulled up a footstool and sat behind the little duke, his long legs stretching out around the child. "I have doubts, Miss Portney, that I can match your talents, but with the aid of some pins I think I could manage a barn." He gave her another of his infuriating smiles.

"By all means, sir," she replied, refusing to be baited into losing her temper again. "Since barns are put together with nails and animals are not, I think that a fair request."

When he threw her a wary look, she wondered what he had taken her remark to mean. She had intended only to be civil, but if he thought her a sufficient wit to couch a barb in such innocent words, she had no wish to apprise him otherwise.

By the time a footman had been sent for Lady Halstead's sewing basket and the desired pins were located, the earl had folded and torn a sheet of paper into an intricate shape.

Everyone watched with fascination as with three pins he attached two walls to make a finished product. In addition to the large barn doors that folded back to open, one side of the hipped roof raised for the arrangement of the animals inside.

"I declare, it is a barn!" Lady Halstead eyed it with lively astonishment. "There is even a door into the hayloft."

"Then we must have a wagon for the hay," Jackie decided.

"Brat, have you no consideration for my fatigue?" Northford gave the duke's shoulder a little shake. "I've made you a barn, can't you be satisfied? And what's the reason for a wagon? You don't have a horse to pull it." His mouth twisted in what Amethy could only consider an arrogant grin—most definitely a challenge.

She accepted. "With or without rider?" she asked airily.

The earl's smile widened. "Without, unless it is now the fashion to use postilions for transporting hay."

Amethy frowned down at the paper in her lap, embarrassed that in her irritation, she had overlooked the obvious.

"One horse, without rider," she announced sharply and went to work furiously. Under her lashes, she saw Northford watch for a moment and then take another scrap of paper. His movements were unhurried, but she gave a slight smile as she saw that his concentration caused furrows between his brows and around his mouth.

Amethy fashioned one horse, laid it aside and quickly made another by the time the wagon was finished. When the earl triumphantly set out his vehicle, she put down first one animal and then another. As she expected, Willy, too, demanded a wagon. She noted with satisfaction the earl's surprise and suddenly lowered brows. The look he threw her said that she had won for the moment, but he was just beginning. He grabbed another sheet of paper and set to work without a word.

By the time the second ingenious wagon had been folded and put together she had three pigs, whereupon Edward wanted a pigsty for their new stock.

"I see your cousin is out to test my skill," Northford said, stroking his chin thoughtfully as he eyed the pigs. "Never let it be said that I ignored a challenge." He favoured Amethy with a glance that seemed more wary than humorous.

Lady Halstead, embroidering a cushion cover for the dining room, was thinking of the reputation of the earl and was distressing herself with her careless stitches as her mind wandered. She cast surreptitious glances at the gentleman who had pushed away the footstool in favour of sitting on the floor. Her niece had appropriated the stool, and she too was closer to the boys as she absorbed herself in fashioning more animals. The worthy matron, who was more admired for her beauty and her love of family than her wit, could not comprehend why the boys found the featureless brown paper animals more interesting than the very expensive set of carved and painted creatures that abounded in the playroom.

Nor could Lady Halstead fathom why her niece and the earl were so engrossed in making them. Her understanding might not be superior, but she could see the frowns on their faces and the looks they cast at one another. It was a contest of sorts, she knew, and deadly serious to both, leaving an aura of tension around the entire room. At first she thought it might be her imagination, but Jackie, too, had noticed it, and he kept biting his lower lip as he watched the two adults from under his long lashes.

The quiet had affected her own boys, though they were oblivious of the contest. Only their sounds as they gave realism to the paper animals broke the silence. It was, therefore, startling to be interrupted by Lord Halstead as he entered the room.

Like Lady Halstead, he was short of stature and rather plump. He was as dark as she was fair, but his disposition was as sunny as hers. His heavily jowled face was most often smiling. At the moment he stood staring down at the clutter on his drawing room floor.

"I say, a neat farm you have there, boys—North-ford! Bless my soul!"

"Hallo, Halstead." The earl rose and shook hands with his host. "Trust you don't mind an addition to your estates."

"Not at all." Kneeling, Halstead picked up a second and more elaborate barn, inspecting it closely.

"An experiment," Northford said as he also knelt. "It occurred to me that I've found a way to show that stupid bailiff of mine what I want built at Wayturn-ing, my place near Leeks. I guess these brats are good for something after all."

"Hmm," Halstead said, nodding, absorbed in the paper structure. "I like it. When you have it built, let me know. Like to ride over and see it. Think I could use these ideas myself." He put the structure on the floor and rose, looking at his wife. "Seems we should be hearing something about luncheon, shouldn't we, Mary?"

Lady Halstead looked at the clock on the mantelpiece and nodded. "It is also time for three little fellows to take themselves up to the nursery for theirs—don't fuss, Willy. You can return to your game later."

When the children had reluctantly filed out of the drawing room, Amethy gathered the papers, putting the animals in one pile, the usable paper in another and the waste scraps together to be taken out by a footman. She still felt uneasy in the slightly amused company of Lord Northford and wished she could have accompanied the boys.

She was grateful that Lord Halstead had engaged the earl's attention. They had each taken a glass of port and walked over to the large windows that gave a view of the copse to the north. Their conversation floated back to where the women sat, as Lord Halstead occupied himself at being host.

"Heard from Seveney the other day that you would be hunting with us this year. Must be pretty tame after the Quorn, eh?"

Northford shrugged. "Shouldn't think so. Terrain looks good, and I've seen some damned fine-looking cattle."

"We're a mixed bag but a game one. The only problem is we've never been able to get Old Sandy." He went on to tell Lord Northford about a wily old fox that kept the hunt at bay. Then he eyed his guest with speculation. "Surprises me you're wintering here, though. Would've thought this area would be a mite too quiet for you."

Under her lashes Amethy saw the amusement before Northford covered it. He turned, raising his voice. "Speaking of wintering—Lady Halstead, I am instructed to extend an invitation from my aunt. Lady Susan would be pleased if you would join us for a winter picnic next week."

"A winter picnic?" Lady Halstead looked up in surprise. "It would be our pleasure, but how can you depend on this odious weather?"

"I have no idea—I'm not privy to the plans," Northford replied. "I was just told the weather, no matter what it is, will be no hindrance."

As the butler chose that moment to announce luncheon, there were no other questions asked about the proposed outing. Luncheon was a quiet meal for Amethy and Lady Halstead. The men discussed the merits of various hunts, though the conversation became one-sided when Lord Halstead launched into a description of the local activities. He was obviously proud of his new position as master of the hunt.

The ladies retired to the drawing room again after the meal was finished and were soon joined by the three young paper farmers. Amethy had made several horses when they decided they must split their buildings into two farms and insisted they needed to ride from one to the other. With her own sewing she joined her aunt at the confidante by the window. They were just seated when they observed Lord Halstead and Lord Northford walking past the window, on their way to the stables.

"Thomas must show off his new hunter," Lady Halstead remarked. "I'm glad of it, I must say. It gets that man out of the house. What a surprise to have Northford bring his ward on a visit." She looked up at Amethy. "I'm sorry to be so blunt, my dear, but I sincerely hope he has not come here because of you."

Amethy was shocked. "Me, ma'am? Until today I had never set eyes on the man! You have convinced me I was in error, but earlier I was persuaded either you or my uncle were trying to arrange an alliance. I confess, my thoughts were quite uncharitable."

Lady Halstead appeared so astounded, Amethy felt moved to explain by telling her aunt of the expressions she had seen on the earl's face. The lady shook her head in wonder.

"I imagine he is much pursued, and while I do not doubt your perceptions, my dear, I cannot think who would be so inclined. Certainly not your uncle or myself, and Lady Susan would never trouble."

"Who is Lady Susan?" Amethy wondered if she had found a culprit to fit her suspicions.

"I disremember exactly—" Using her needle, Lady Halstead sketched a pattern in the air as if stitching her memories together. "Jackie's great-aunt—once removed up the family tree, I think. Yes, that's right."

"Who is she then?" Amethy was having trouble following her aunt's logic.

"She's the younger daughter of the seventh Duke— our little fellow's grandfather would have been her brother." Lady Halstead allowed herself a triumphant smile. "She and Northford seem to get on very well together."

Like Amethy, Lady Halstead was a Portney, and was given to the mental tenacity of the line. Once finished with the tangential question, she immediately returned to the main problem occupying her mind.

"Are you positive, you have never met Northford in London?"

"I am convinced," Amethy asserted. "And I much doubt he knew of my existence until he entered this room. Nor did I have any idea he was the child's guardian. I confess the thought distresses me. Little Jackie could be better circumstanced, for all his rank."

Lady Halstead turned thoughtful. "So it seemed to me at the time, but I've since wondered."

"Surely you don't approve?" Amethy could but wonder that her aunt, so sensitive to her own children's welfare, could ignore the unfortunate circumstances of little Jackie.

"The earl's attachment to the child has surprised the neighbourhood—he spends a goodly amount of time with the boy—more than many fathers do," Amethy's aunt explained. "We thought he'd carry the child to London or one of his properties if he continued his interest, but it's said he feels a Duke of Lowestroft should be raised in his ancestral home."

"There must be more to the story," Amethy said, not willing to credit the earl with these finer feelings.

"I daresay." Lady Halstead's eyes twinkled. "I hear his aunt, Lady Rachel, is ensconced at Severton Manor, his principal seat and nothing would induce her to leave it. My mother used to speak of her—a terrible old dragon." The twinkle turned to surprise and wonder. "My goodness, Lady Rachel must be nearly ninety!"

"Is she Lady Susan's sister?" Amethy was always interested in the intricacies of intertwining kinship.

"On, no, the connexion between the Farringhams and the Marlings is quite distant, relating back to the fifth duke, I believe, and then on the maternal side."

"But the child calls Northford cousin," Amethy objected. She had a high regard for her aunt's grasp of family ties, but something was clearly amiss.

"I'm persuaded the kinship is exaggerated for the child's sake." Lady Halstead was in no way discomfited by her niece's doubts. "The true tie between them isn't blood, but Northford's friendship with Jackie's late father. The earl and the ninth duke were great friends—so unlikely, too, because a more staid and responsible man than Justin Farringham, I've yet to meet." Amethy's aunt paused to raise the embroidery hoop and consider her work. When she lowered it, she gazed out across the room deep in thought.

"I suppose the late duke knew Northford better than the rest of us. He left the boy in his care and that trust seems not to have been misplaced. He is more and more often at Lowestroft."

"He's likely in the basket," Amethy remarked, and seeing the inquiring look from her aunt she explained. "His purse is probably empty."

"Oh, that I've never heard. It is said he's excessively wealthy. I only know from gossip, of course, but Thomas tells me his properties are all in good aspect. We may not approve of his escapades, but Thomas says the earl's no fool."

Amethy shook her head. "Well, I cannot like the way he speaks to the child, calling him a brat and a beast, and within the child's hearing, too. It shows a want of affection."

Lady Halstead let her embroidery rest in her lap as she looked across the room at the children, busy with the new toys.

"I'm unconvinced by his words. Men show affection to boys in the most peculiar ways. I thought it showed great feeling that he assisted in their game. If, as you say, it was not because of you he came, then it must have been because of the child. I'm of a much better opinion of him for it."

Amethy frowned at her aunt. "I can only repeat that I have never met the man until today, and for my part, it is not an acquaintance I would wish to further. I'm of the belief that he came to discuss the hunt with Lord Halstead, and his part in the game was only an attempt to make me look foolish after the set-down I gave him. I doubt he had the children in mind at all.'' She picked up her sewing, set a stitch and dropped the work into her lap. "At the risk of seeming quite rude, I hope I may be excused from attending a picnic in November—I am convinced it cannot be at all comfortable.''

"But you cannot refuse, my dear,'' Lady Halstead objected, gazing on her niece with a look akin to panic. "We must not offend him, lest the ill feeling carry into the future; theirs is a powerful family.'' She dropped her sewing and clasped her plump hands together. "The thought of spending a day in the company of Lady Susan without your support leaves me in terror. Who would have planned this picnic I cannot guess—certainly not Lady Susan. She is the most vague and absentminded woman imaginable. On the few occasions she has visited me I have been singularly uncomfortable. She stares into space, and I know she doesn't hear a word said to her. Most disconcerting!''

Amethy vouchsafed no answer and continued with her sewing until Jackie left the other boys and came to sit beside her. The child was quiet for some minutes before she realized he was leaning heavily against her shoulder, asleep. She put aside her work and tilted him on his side, allowing him to lie across her lap. With one sturdy little arm crooked and his cheek pressed against it, he gave a contented sigh and relaxed.

She thought it too unfortunate that he had neither mother nor father, but only the earl to care for him, believing he would get precious little affection from that quarter. Thinking of the mocking smile and the cool, amused eyes, she pursed her lips in irritation. Such a man had no right to such a beautiful child.

Some time later the gentlemen returned to the room, and Jackie was still sleeping. Lord Northford's expression was enigmatic as he observed his ward lying sprawled across Amethy's lap. He came forward to stand looking down at the child.

"A bold little man is my cousin. But I'll have to remove him from such delightful company. The weather threatens and we should be on our way."

Northford's voice awakened Jackie who sat up, rubbing his eyes with one fist. "Must we go? I like it here," he said sleepily.

"I don't doubt it," the earl replied, his lips curling slightly as he gazed at Amethy.

"I don't want to leave yet," Jackie complained again, leaning back against the back of the confidante.

Instead of arguing with the child, Northford walked across the room and settled himself comfortably in a chair, speaking to his ward dispassionately.

"Very well, but I think it will rain soon. We can either leave now and ride back on Thunder or wait until the rain starts and accept the loan of a carriage from Lord Halstead."

The threat of returning home in a carriage instead of riding with his cousin brought the little duke up from the couch in a bound. He hurriedly made his farewells, tugging at the earl's hand to get him back on his feet. He only took time to admonish Edward and Willy to bring the paper farm when they came for the picnic.

The earl was slower in taking his leave. He shook hands with his host, and bowed to his hostess and to Amethy with elaborate correctness.

"We will look forward to seeing you at Lowestroft," he murmured. "I hope in the meantime you will not allow yourself to be carried away. It would break my cousin's heart."

Amethy, still sensitive to the wary look she'd seen in his eye when he first arrived, took his remark to mean that he still held to his suspicion. She desired above all things to give him a severe set-down, but her strict training prevented it.

"Have no fear, sir, I will be there," she answered him in frigid tones.

After he had taken the child and departed, she stood at the window watching him ride down the drive with Jackie on the saddle before him. Insufferable, well-mannered boor, she thought him, and wondered how the ladies of London could sigh over such a haughty, insolent creature.

She would admit he was handsome, and his address was well polished. Just like a stone that has been smoothed by the waters of a stream, she thought.

"Amethy, I wish you will not think about him too much," Lady Halstead commented as if she had been reading her niece's mind. "He may show himself in a good light when he's with his ward, but consider what we know about him."

"Aunt Mary! I was not thinking about that odious man!" Amethy returned to the confidante and picked up her sewing, hoping her flaming cheeks were hidden by the light at her back.

CHAPTER THREE

"FEATHERBRAINED!" Nurse Kerns pronounced, the strength of her emotions overriding her usual carefully patterned speech. "Mark my words, no good will come of my lady jaunting about the countryside in her condition."

Amethy, somewhat fatigued with the good woman's dark prophecies, chose not to answer. She was sure her aunt knew what she was about, and when the newest addition to the family could be expected. Amethy turned her attention to Edward and Willy who were busily planning a day of high adventure.

"And towers," Willy was saying to his brother, his red curls bobbing as he bounced in his excitement. "Maybe they lock people up in the towers and chop their heads off, and there's blood on the floor, and running down the steps and—"

Edward nodded slowly, his eyes large at the thought.

"Stuff!" cried Nurse Kerns. "I hardly think Lord Northford, for all his rakish..." Her sensibilities sorely tried by the journey, the nurse had said more than she intended and caught herself a fraction too late. She looked imploringly at the young lady by her side, silently asking her to draw the attention of the boys from her gaffe.

"I think towers must be more exciting than anything," Amethy said with hurried brightness, and in her effort to come to the nurse's rescue, realized she was encouraging the subject deplored by her harried companion. She sought for a middle of the road substitution.

"Even if there are no people locked in them," she added quickly. "For you must know that chopping off heads is not at all the thing. Surely our friend the duke is better mannered than that."

"Sometimes he forgets to say 'thank-you,'" Willy reminded her, not quite willing to give up the fascinating horror he had so forcefully painted.

Edward pulled at the lock of dark blond hair that habitually fell over his forehead and appeared to be his handle on ideas. "Maybe they torture people in the dungeon," he offered, seeking to reinstate the adventure offered at Lowestroft by suggesting a new idea.

"There are dungeons," Willy told Amethy, reinforcing his brother. "Maybe they feed people to the dragon that lives down there."

"Possibly," Amethy said, seeming to give the idea some thought. "And I think it must be the most horrible thing ever, to be eaten by a dragon." She shivered, wrapping her arms about herself. She had no doubt there would be cellars under Lowestroft and even natural caves. There were famous caverns in the area, and limestone was a feature of the hilly countryside. Her shivers were an attempt to engender in the boys a fear of trying to find any.

"What a silly idea," Nurse Kerns objected. "Where you boys get such ideas, I'll never know." She turned a fulminating eye on Amethy, but the young lady was not cowed. It could hardly harm the children to hear tales of brave deeds from long ago, even if she did at times concoct them from her lively imagination and love of chivalry.

Neither Edward nor Willy gave much attention to their nurse's opinions, since she obviously did not understand adventure as did their cousin. They followed Amethy's example and shivered. Then Willy's new chivalry broke the surface of his imagination.

"If the dragon gets you, we'll save you, Amethy."

"Thank you, Willy. I feel so much safer, knowing you'll protect me." Amethy wondered how she was to extricate herself from the imaginative conversation of which the nurse so heartily disapproved.

"We'll find a magic thword," Edward lisped, smiling at his brother. Normally Willy was the one to put forth the imaginative ideas. Edward's slower, more plodding mind seldom showed the sparkle of his younger brother, though in Edward's defence, he was at times able to take Willy's ideas and convert them into workable plans, completely oversetting the family's comfort. But at the moment he was pleased with himself for adding to the romance of the proposed adventure, and Willy was generous enough to give him a nod of approval.

"Oh, yes," Amethy agreed. "You must find a magic sword, for no one could fight a dragon without one, and no great hero, no matter how brave, would ever go near such a creature without one."

Amethy, had been an imaginative child and remembered how she had been able to ignore the dreary and logical warnings of adults. As she fully expected, both boys took this bit of nonsense quite seriously. It carried all the weight of practicality found in starlight and fairies dancing within magic circles.

The boys' conversation turned to the problem of where to find that piece of special equipment needed to carry out their brave deeds—and Amethy leaned back against the seat, satisfied now that the direction of their thoughts had been turned. They would surely be disappointed, she thought, because Lowestroft was more likely just some manor house with a presumptuous name. It was not listed in any of the guide books, and if it was accounted a seat of some great repute, she had never heard it spoken of in Society.

When the carriage topped a rise, it occurred to Amethy that if Lowestroft were not well-known, the reason lay with its owners' desire for privacy and not its lack of worth as a show place. She looked down into a depression between the hills and gazed upon a true castle in the ancient sense. The outer walls, the bastions and the towers lacked the grace of imitative structures; they were thickly built and bulky in their ancient defensive proportions. The evenness of the ground around the keep gave evidence that in some past years a moat had been filled in.

Like the children, she stared with the fascination achieved only when reality overcame expectation. Through her mind passed a childish thrill; there would be dungeons.

As the carriage drew closer and passed within the outer wall, the only incongruity of the imposing and ancient structure appeared to be the windows, clearly not in the style of defence. The small panes and leading indicated that their addition had been during the sixteenth century. Knowing how dark the castle must have been without them, Amethy felt the addition clearly justified.

If the castle itself was a surprise, no less so was the welcome afforded by the servants to the second carriage of the Halstead party. The butler sailed out accompanied by a fleet of footmen, and by their solicitous ushering of the guests into the building, accorded them all the importance of a visit from the Regent himself.

They were led down confusing passages through a myriad of rooms, quite opulent, Amethy thought, for the ground floor. Like the children's, her eyes strayed to the suits of armour, ancient banners and the many evidences of a long and active line of the duke's ancestors.

At last they were taken through an impressive doorway where the butler strove to announce them, though he was overborne in volume as Willy reacted to their surroundings.

"It's an inside outside," the child shrilled.

While Willy's description might have been ambiguous to someone not seeing the room of quite magnificent proportions, he was in fact, succinct and to the point. No effort had been spared to convert the interior into a garden. Numerous exotic potted plants and trees, doubtless brought in to protect them from the cold, had been placed to create the atmosphere of a formal garden. Interspersed among them, flowering plants, no doubt from the greenhouse, added colour with their bright blooms.

At one end of the long room, a small pen had been fashioned, and within it an ewe and a lamb looked on the newcomers with placid eyes. Close by, a number of low wooden tubs were clustered, and upon the smooth surface of the water within them, a large white duck, followed by a brood of four yellow ducklings, swam in lazy circles.

At the other end of the room, quite surrounded by tall shrubs and giving the appearance of a summer house, a lattice framework encircled an arrangement of garden furniture. Most jarring to the garden effect was a fire blazing in the large hearth, but the chill of the day made that one incongruity not only forgivable, but welcome.

By the windows, giving onto a view of the garden, four gentlemen were engaged in conversation; two of them immediately recognizable to Amethy as her uncle and Lord Northford. The other two were strangers. Seated near the fire, a lady of regal bearing was staring into the fire, seemingly ignoring Lady Halstead, who was, from what Amethy could ascertain from a distance, trying to maintain a polite monologue in lieu of regular conversation.

Amethy was just turning in their direction when she was accosted by Jackie, who came skipping across the sand and rushes spread upon the floor.

"Did you bring the paper farm?" he demanded of Willy and Edward as he caught Amethy's hand. Then remembering his manners, he stepped back to make his leg and then grasped her fingers again.

"Miss Amethy, come see Fluffy! He is my very own sheep, and mine to take care of and everything!" He tugged at her arm, pulling her in the direction of the small pen.

"You have a sheep of your very own?" Willy queried, his awe evident as the two Halstead boys followed Jackie and Amethy across the floor.

"I'm going to take care of him and love him and he will be the biggest and beautifulest sheep that ever was,'' Jackie said as he climbed between the railings and pushed the little creature closer to the makeshift fence. "You can pet him if you want to, Miss Amethy," he said shyly.

Sensible of her duty, Amethy stroked the small woolly head. "I think it is ever so nice to have a lamb as a pet!" she exclaimed, hoping she had exhibited the proper enthusiasm, though why Lord Northford would give a lamb into the noble child's care was beyond her understanding.

Since in her initial opinion of the earl she had been most disapproving, she found herself trying to put even this gift in an unsavoury light, but she was hard pressed to do so. The quite excellent care of the properties, as seen from the carriage, the superb condition of the castle, both without and within, and the amount of effort put out to provide a social engagement suitable to include the children, spoke of a careful guardianship she had not quite believed.

The knowledge that she was seeking some disapproval by which to keep the man's charm from affecting her helped not at all.

But the unspoken question that had prompted her reverie was asked aloud by Edward, who along with his brother, had climbed into the pen. The little duke's answer gave Amethy the wedge she had been seeking.

"My cousin says I'll learn something about animals," Jackie was explaining. "He says 'damn I grow up to be a park saunter...saun—'"

The wedge, however, was quite effectively nullified by the both plaintive and resigned voice that came from behind her.

"Brat, must you be forever repeating what you're not supposed to hear?"

Having on several occasions dissolved into the most exquisite embarrassment by having her unthinking words repeated by her small cousins, Amethy could only feel sympathy for the lord caught in a similar situation.

Her blue-violet eyes that gave rise to her name were brimming with laughter when she turned to face her host.

Despite the humour, she felt a frisson of delight pass through her as she looked up into his handsome, aristocratic face. She understood why many females could sigh over him, though his reputation entirely put off a person of taste and sensibility.

Again he exhibited a nicety of taste in his dress as a country gentleman. Though his wine coat did not affect a fit requiring a valet and two footmen to help him to put it on, still, the unmistakable hand of an exclusive London tailor could be seen in the style and cut.

No student of fashion in tying of men's neckcloths, Amethy nevertheless noted the snowy folds tucking themselves around his collar. In London, she had on occasion overheard several men of fashion speaking of their efforts to achieve the "Desmond," as they termed Northford's way of arranging his cravat. She was surprised to note that while precise, the effect was not at all flamboyant.

Northford gave her a perfect leg, and with a flip of his thumb, opened his snuff box.

"I trust you had a pleasant trip from Halstead Manor?"

"Quite, thank you." Amethy, remembering his attitude on his visit to Halstead Manor, was determined to give him no cause to think she would put any undue value on his company. She turned away to gaze at the children within the pen.

"I fear you have lost your ardent admirer," he said, looking over at the pen and the children. "My cousin appears the flighty type. A lamb with the most imaginative name of Fluffy has, I think, usurped even your place in his affection."

She raised her brows as if in surprise. "But how not, sir, for I am convinced no lovelier creature could exist—and as for the lack of originality in the name, is imagination a necessary trait for one destined by all appearances to become a noble farmer?"

Northford raised a negligent hand, as if waving away some lingering insect. "A sheepherder—not even I am so unfeeling as to put my ward behind the plow until he's at least six."

Amethy felt he was trying to catch her with some hidden meaning, though she could not fathom what it would be. To prevent it, she chose a safer subject.

"I compliment both you and your aunt on your original idea. Your winter picnic promises to be quite pleasant."

The earl's eyes flickered again as another, ambiguous emotion showed briefly in them. "Somehow I doubt your credit is properly placed," he said, his voice carrying a hint of a thoughtful question.

"I'm afraid I don't understand." She was caught by the unexpectedness of his reaction to a simple compliment.

"I had nothing to do with the concept, and I cannot envision Lady Susan planning this affair." His voice, already low, dropped as he leaned his head towards hers. "I confess to be fascinated. I live in momentary expectancy of some thrilling new adventure.

We may even be enthralled by dogcart rides around the room.''

So totally unexpected was Northford's suggestion, that Amethy forgot her wariness of the man and choked back a gasp of laughter. ''You cannot be serious.''

''Most dreadfully serious. But there's hope that we may experience something even more exciting. I sincerely hope you will not take it personally if I find myself in the position of challenging your ability to herd geese down the room?''

''Not at all, sir. I am persuaded I can herd geese as well as the august Earl of Northford.'' She gave him an arch smile. ''And no doubt, I have as much experience as you.''

Folding his arms across his chest, his look down his well-shaped nose was one of knowing hauteur. ''I doubt it. Once, while travelling across France I had the—shall we say—the fascinating task of fending for myself on a strange road in a storm. The only shelter I found was a hovel, overloaded with the honking monsters. Since I had the choice of sleeping with them or getting them out, I learned geese herding with dispatch.''

Amethy, for years an unwilling ear to Lord Northford's colourful and quite rakish past, found it almost ludicrous to hear such an unromantic if strangely charming story of his travels. A sudden vision of him, dressed in the best of London and Paris, wearing gleaming Hessians while he struggled to remove a number of recalcitrant geese from their abode, brought out a trill of laughter.

The earl seemed to enjoy her mirth, and the smile it vouchsafed from him was indeed charming and for once seemed quite sincere. Amethy's laughter died in the strange sensation that the smile was having upon her, causing her to catch her breath. But the look was short-lived. His eyes raised from her face to look beyond her, and she noted his start of surprise as he gazed towards the door.

Amethy turned and espied three people just entering the room behind the butler who announced,

"Lord and Lady Battenton and Miss Ruth Oglethorpe."

Northford's brows, which had been raised in inquiry, as if asking if she believed his outrageous tale, snapped down as if in irritation. For a moment he appeared to be displeased with the entrance of the new arrivals, but the look was masked so quickly Amethy was not sure she had read it correctly.

He made his excuse and went forward to greet his new guests.

As the earl crossed the floor, Amethy let her gaze rest on the strangers as long as courtesy would allow. The gentleman, she noted, was some half a head shorter than Lord Northford. His narrow shoulders were thrown back as if to give himself a chest but only succeeded in emphasizing his lack of sturdy build. His clothing smacked of the dandy, and his manner of elevating his nose, as if to rise above something unpleasant, suggested that he was used to being better placed. Obviously he viewed himself far more seriously and certainly of more importance than the world in general regarded him. A bore, she thought and dismissed him from her thoughts.

Though two females had been introduced, there was no doubt about which one bore the title of Lady Battenton. Short of height, her most excessive weight was added to by the style of clothing she affected, the many shawls and scarves winding about her voluminous person, and the quite ludicrous ostrich feathers she wore pinned in her elaborate hairstyle. Behind her, the young woman dressed with taste, without being ostentatious, faded into the background.

Approaching the new arrivals, Northford held out his hand to Lord Battenton. The conversation drifted back to Amethy.

"Hallo, Henry, thought by now you would have been hung."

"Hardly, old fellow, since I gave up your tricks years ago."

"Elvira, you look to be in the pink of health."

Amethy, turning back to watch the children playing with the lamb, could imagine the earl's perfect bow.

"Well, I'm glad I look it, because you may believe I don't feel well at all," the highly pitched voice of Lady Battenton whined across the room. "My health is not at all good, and if it were not for the affection I feel for you and the dear child, I would not have made the effort to come. And I can tell you it was an effort—why they don't do something about the roads I cannot fathom. When a person of delicacy must make a journey—I say nothing of myself, but poor Ruth..."

"Gad, Elvira, you sound as if we travelled from India!" Lord Battenton's irritation carried no hint of a desire for discretion.

Amethy, caught between her embarrassment at having overheard the conversation and her dislike of public bickering, sought release in letting her eyes roll to the ceiling. But when her gaze again fell to the level of her own head, she blushed with shame. Behind a clump of potted shrubs, she saw, watching her, one of the Lowestroft people, a groom, by his clothing. She was just about to turn away when his slight nod and almost imperceptible smile showed his complete agreement with her feelings.

Courtesy demanded that Amethy present herself to her hostess, for she had been in the room some ten minutes, either engaged by Jackie or Lord North-ford. She crossed the room, not at all anxious to approach Lady Susan after hearing of the good woman's idiosyncrasies. Nor did she wish to enter the company of Lord and Lady Battenton, if their small contretemps was an indication of their company manners.

The gentlemen, too, were approaching the other end of the room, and like Amethy, somewhat reluctantly. With so many people who had not met one another, the introductions became involved and lengthy, but Amethy was interested to meet General Duckworth, whose military bearing did nothing to hide his elfin quality. He was a round little man whose baby-pink face had elongated to include the top of his head. His snowy white hair grew thickly over his ears. Amethy was struck by the similarity of his appearance to a shoemaker elf in a book she had loved as a child.

With the general was his grandson, a young man who had, because of the thinning out of the family, just succeeded to the title of Viscount Edgemere. He seemed to be a bit abashed by both his new position and the present company, and his eyes darted about as if searching for some safe shelter. His round chinless face combined with his sharp sudden movements to put Amethy in mind of a squirrel.

Lady Battenton lowered herself into a chair next to Amethy's aunt and at once started to decry the day, the journey, and in moments had worked the subject around to the unique arrangement of the room.

"I declare, I cannot think what Susan is about." She pulled a fan from her reticule and started to fan herself vigorously after having chosen the chair nearest the fire. "I am much appalled that she would bring her guests into a room with green rushes on the floor. I am certain that to sit here will be most injurious to Ruth's constitution, though I won't speak of my own weaknesses. So delicate you know, though you would hardly guess it to look at me. I think I must ask Susan, for Ruth's sake, if we can adjourn to another part of the house when I am feeling more the thing..."

Lady Halstead, clearly not knowing how to answer such an outrageous breach of etiquette, looked at Amethy for inspiration. But the need for her assistance was eliminated by General Duckworth, who glowered down at the complainer.

"Understand this is a winter picnic...the room was especially arranged for our pleasure...like it myself." Having made his statement, he further exhibited his support of the scheme by taking himself over to sit by Lady Susan.

There were an unlikely pair, Amethy thought, comparing the general's elfin quality to Lady Susan's aristocratic reserve. Though their hostess sat relaxed, Amethy sensed an illusion of iron stiffness, not lessened by the carefully arranged grey hair and the high-bridged nose over a pair of thin lips.

"Well, I never!" Lady Battenton lowered her voice, though it carried all the indignity of a shout. "What can Susan and Northford be thinking of, having people like that about? I can only hope Ruth is charitable in her thoughts about the company she must suffer here.''

It was on Amethy's lips to say she found the general quite a delightful person, but persuaded nothing would be accomplished by matching Lady Battenton's bad manners, she kept her thoughts to herself. She allowed her gaze to travel in Miss Oglethorpe's direction and saw that the young woman had overheard and was indeed suffering, but from a most exquisite embarrassment at being used as a ploy.

Ruth Oglethorpe looked as if she wanted to shrink into the floor, and Amethy couldn't help but think the girl lived with that unenviable attitude. Her clothes, plain and of undistinguished colour, though well made and of good material, bespoke a desire to be overlooked. Her heart-shaped face was pretty, but her hair was drawn back in a plain and unbecoming knot at the nape of her neck.

Amethy could not help but pity the girl, but even these thoughts were chased away by Willy as he dashed across the room and up to her, holding something dark in his tight little fist.

"Amethy! Look, I found a lizard," he said, holding out his hand, offering his prize to the young lady for inspection. Sympathetic as she might be to the adventures of the boys, lizards were not her favourite creatures. She would have liked to say "How nice," and removed herself from the immediate company with dispatch, but the little face smiling so happily into hers forbade any such cowardly action.

Behind Willy, Edward and Jackie were approaching, Edward carrying the mother duck, and the ducklings followed. It would never do for the boys to bring the creatures over in the company of Lady Battenton, so Amethy determined to admire the lizard, the duck and get the children back to the other side of the room. Obviously the nurses were of the same opinion, since both Nurse Kerns and Nurse Rae had noticed the boys' direction and were coming in hot pursuit.

Amethy was tentatively extending her hand, shrinking from the expected contact with what she could only think of as slimy and reptilian, when Lady Battenton took the matter entirely out of her control.

"A lizard!" she ejaculated, and threw up her hands. Her reticule, attached to her left wrist by its ribbons, struck both Willy's and Amethy's hands as he was in the act of handing her his find, therefore neither of them had a firm grip. As luck would have it, the dark object flew into the air and landed in Lady Battenton's lap. With a scream she heaved her prodigious weight from the chair and proceeded to go into hysterics.

This startled both Edward and the duck he was carrying. The duck struggled, and the child dropped the creature, who immediately ran under the feet of a footman just bringing in a large tray on which reposed a number of silver dishes containing the first course for their picnic lunch.

The footman, stumbling over the duck, dropped the tray, and the result was a ringing of silver dishes accompanied by a reverberating gong from the large tray as it struck one of the empty chairs. The ringing clatter of the falling serving pieces were only an addition to Lady Battenton's hysterics, Willy's wail, Edward and Jackie crying out that the footman might step on the frightened ducklings and the squawking mama duck. The racket threw the ewe into such terror that she broke out of the pen and raced across the floor with the lamb following, bleating pitifully.

The little duke, seeing his new pet, Fluffy, racing across the room, started after the lamb, followed by Nurse Rae, who cried out her fears that her little gentleman could be trampled by the maddened sheep.

As if her words had been prophecy, they nearly came to pass. As Jackie, closely followed by the nurse, reached the lamb, the ewe, realizing she had outrun the distance her offspring could manage in the same time, turned back, her new direction taking her on a collision course with Nurse Rae. As the two collided, the good nurse slid on the rushes and one leg doubled back under her. She fell with a scream of pain, quite loud enough to bring a halt to the major cacophony going on in the room. In the comparative quiet that followed, Willy's sniffles were intermingled with the quacking of the duck as she gathered her ducklings under her wing, and the hysteria of Lady Battenton, which was cut off in midsentence by Lady Susan. The hostess had sufficiently roused herself to give the stout woman a sound shake.

For moments everyone stood or sat, quite frozen by the happenings. Then Lord Northford turned to Amethy.

"I beg your pardon, Miss Portney," he drawled; his nonchalance was ludicrous after the chaos. "I fear there will be no dogcart rides. Quite bland after this bit of entertainment, don't you think?" He then strolled over to where Nurse Rae lay on the floor. She was trying to stifle her moans of pain and was being comforted by Nurse Kerns.

While Northford's remark elicited nothing from Amethy but a blank stare, it released the tension among the male adults who, one and all, began to laugh. Even the footman, picking up the dishes, saw the earl's eyes pass over him without censure and so forgot himself as to smile before he remembered his training and turned blank-faced again. The mirth was short lived, because as the party realized the direction of Lord Northford's course, the thought of the nurse's injury sobered everyone.

Only Lady Battenton appeared to have more concern for the incident than the nurse's plight. She turned to harangue both Amethy and Willy for the intrusion into the gathering of a lizard. Her condemnation brought renewed tears from the child, who plainly considered himself the injured party. He glowered up at the stout woman.

"You threw away my lizard! Now I can't find it."

Amethy, feeling the child's outrage somewhat justified, tried to pacify him.

"Dear, it just ran away and hid, I am convinced we'll find it. And if we do not, it will return to its home and be perfectly happy there."

"But it couldn't run away!" Willy's voice shrilled. "It was only a pretend lizard!"

The child's admission had the effect of catching most of the party with their mouths at half-cock. Even the urbane Lord Northford, heading now in the direction of the still-kneeling footman, after seeing to the nurse, was brought up at half stride. As if to prove the point, Lord Edgemere stepped forward, knelt and retrieved an object from the floor.

Willy moved forward to take it, but before relinquishing the object the young gentleman held it up so all and sundry could see a piece of wood, obviously a long thick splinter off one of the water tubs where the ducks had been swimming. The irregularities did quite remarkably resemble a small, harmless reptile native to the area.

"Actually, it could not have been real," said the viscount, handing the splinter back to the child. "At this season, lizards hibernate."

That bit of information brought a look of contempt from Lord Battenton, and since it was most clearly directed at Lady Battenton, she immediately expostulated on Ruth's nerves, though she would not mention her own delicate condition and how it was unthinkable to allow even the semblance of such a creature around persons of extreme sensibilities.

"Elvira, will you cease!" demanded Lord Northford with such sudden force, that it brought all sound to a halt again. He quite soundly shocked everyone in the room, particularly when his gaze was found to be, not on the woman creating more furor, but upon Lady Halstead.

"Aunt Mary!" Amethy cried as she turned to look at her aunt. The dear woman was sitting quite still, her hands gripping the arms of the chair. The whiteness around her mouth could only indicate severe pain. Gradually both the paleness and the tension seemed to leave her, and she looked up at Lord Halstead. She spoke somewhat breathlessly, though she was very calm.

"Thomas, dear, I'm afraid you must make our excuses."

"Lord, Mary, not now!" Lord Halstead seemed staggered as he took in the import of her words.

"Yes, dear. I very much fear it is now. Please call for the carriage."

Lord Halstead, turning to do his wife's bidding, was stopped by Lord Northford by the simple expedient of catching the expectant father's arm. Northford's objections to the plan were clipped and forceful.

"Man, what are you thinking of? It's seven miles back to Halstead Manor, will you risk having your child born on the side of the road?"

Lord Halstead was brought to his senses. He shook his head. "No. Wasn't thinking. Mustn't bounce Mary about in a carriage just now."

"A message is now on the way to Doctor Campbell, telling him to come here." Northford indicated the nurse who was at that moment being lifted from the floor by three footmen. "Her leg seems to be broken," he added, as if his concern for a servant might need some explanation.

"Well, I shall certainly want to see him as soon as he arrives," Lady Battenton announced. "My nerves cannot take much more of this hurly-burly."

Lady Susan roused herself to the circumstances. In a few clipped sentences, she had ordered the footman to carry Nurse Rae to the servants' quarters on the ground level, where she would be more easily cared for than in the nursery. Rooms were ordered prepared for all the Halstead party, the first, of course, for Lady Halstead.

A pale but steady Lord Halstead carried his wife from the room. Nurse Kerns sailed out in his wake, wearing that particularly triumphant air only attained by having her darkest predictions justified.

Lady Susan sat for a moment, then on rising, suggested to Lady Battenton that she might prefer to rest in one of the rooms being made up. The stout woman, gratified by the attention, followed Lady Susan from the room.

Their host gestured towards the butler, who had entered the room and stood staring at the debris left by the recent panic as if he had never envisioned such a disaster in a place where he ruled.

"Tilbin..." Lord Northford paused, as if, now that he had the servant's attention, he was unsure of his wishes. He indicated the damage with a negligent hand.

"I fear a small incident has rendered this room quite inappropriate as a place for luncheon. Have you any suggestions?"

The butler drew himself up. "I agree, my lord, and if I may suggest, a buffet in the dining room would maintain the informality of the occasion and be so much—" he looked around "—neater."

"Dear me, do we really want more informality?" Northford gently complained. "For my part I think I have had enough of nature—and its results."

"If I may be so bold, sir, I think you would find it wise," Tilbin answered.

The attitude of pleasant nonchalance at once fell away from Lord Northford and his eyes narrowed. "How so?"

To maintain his aplomb in the face of his master's disapproval apparently required further puffing up on Tilbin's part, but like a fluffed feather bed after a night of its occupant's tossing and turning, he deflated again.

"My lord, it is often noticed that in a household in which a happy occasion is imminent, the females of the household, from the housekeeper to the lowest scullery maid, are instantly raised above their stations—''

"Cut line!'' Northford ordered, his eyes turning slate coloured with his irritation. "Are you saying the discipline of the household staff is breaking down?''

Tilbin's gaze sought and found the ceiling. "Has broken down, my lord, and even my footmen have been recruited to carry hot water.''

It could not be thought wonderful if such a person as the Earl of Northford had, upon learning his comfort was being overset, reacted in a manner most uncomfortable to the butler, but in fact, Northford threw back his head and laughed.

"Very well, a buffet it must be, but both for the comfort of Lady Halstead and ourselves, we all wish her a short travail.''

Amethy had taken a seat close to the fire, and the three children, at a loss since both their nurses had been taken from them, had gathered close to her. As Tilbin looked in their direction, he was apparently struck by their presence.

"And shall I get the nursery maid to come for the little gentlemen, my lord?''

As Northford's attention turned to the children, they pressed closer to Amethy. It was in her mind to say she would remove them to the nursery, but before the words could be uttered, the earl shook his head in a most definite decision.

"With the uproar above stairs, better they remain here with us.'' He considered the children a second time. "And Tilbin, if I understand correctly, a rather important brown paper parcel was expected to arrive at the same time as the Halstead party. It might have been carried in, or perhaps it arrived on its own in a brown paper wagon, pulled by a brown paper horse—"

his eye sought Amethy's as the children giggled at the picture he presented "—without rider."

"I do remember such a parcel, sir," the butler answered, his dignity softened by a slight crinkle in his cheeks, though his lips remained straight.

"Then have it delivered to the green drawing room while we are at luncheon."

The party that partook of the buffet luncheon was a good deal more subdued at the beginning of the meal than it had been before the series of accidents. With the arrival of Lord Halstead, interest quickened. When he attempted to forgo luncheon, he was immediately beset by demands to keep up his strength.

He was persuaded to eat, but his sensibility of the inconvenience to his host was lowering to his spirit.

"Dashed inconsiderate of us, bringing our troubles and putting you out," he told Northford. "Mary had no idea, of course. Better wife and mother a man couldn't ask for, but a bit addled when it comes to dates and things. Never has got this increase thing right."

Amethy, feeling most acutely the suffering of her uncle, gave Lord Northford an arch look.

"I am persuaded it is Lowestroft that is in our debt," she announced. "Who else is considerate enough to bring such excitement into the life of even the scullery maids?"

"Just so," Northford replied, accepting the statement and amplifying it. "And I'm still convinced Willy's lizard saved us from dogcart rides, which is no mean accomplishment."

Around the table, several people laughed, and Amethy's attention was drawn to those who did not. Miss Oglethorpe and Lord Edgemere were engaged in their own conversation and apparently had not heard the sallies. She had not thought about it before, but during the calm periods in the picnic hall, they had been together, apart from the rest of the company. Lord Battenton was engaged in frowning at the absorbed couple, and he, too, had missed the humour of the situation.

Three others had neglected to laugh. The children, so proud to be taking luncheon with the adults, were being little models of well-bred silence. But their appetites had been satisfied. They were fatigued by all the excitement and had fallen asleep in their chairs.

"I suppose they're for the nursery after all," Northford said as he noticed the direction of Amethy's attention.

"Poor little things," Amethy said, nodding in agreement. "I'll go up with them."

"No such thing," Lord Halstead objected. "I'll take them—at least Willy."

"And I'll take our brat," Northford said as he rose. "Be hard on the little blighter, with the nurse out of action." He looked around and turned to call a footman who was removing the dishes. With the energy of the young, Viscount Edgemere volunteered. He jumped to his feet, his quick movements nearly oversetting the chair.

When the three gentlemen left the room with the children, Lord Battenton rose and turned to Amethy, his hauteur so thick it could almost be seen in the air.

"Doubtless you are worried about your aunt. Perhaps a game of whist would settle your nerves." He sounded as if he were conveying some high honour on her.

Amethy would have been undecided whether to take offense or laugh if her mind had not been taken up with other matters.

"Forgive me, but I think I must check on my aunt, then speak with my uncle when he returns from the nursery," she said, rising. "We must decide what's to be done."

General Duckworth, at the other end of the table, was engaged in a one-sided conversation with Lady Susan and showed no desire for a game of cards, so Lord Battenton rose from the table and went out of the room.

Amethy, not allowed to enter the room where her aunt lay, was assured she was bearing up under her travail. The young lady was in search of her uncle when she passed Lord Battenton in the passage. For a moment she thought he wished to speak to her, but a servant was detaining him with a question and was receiving a very short answer.

HAD THEY BEEN in London, the ladies and gentlemen then staying in Lowestroft would have been engaged in various social activities hardly begun at ten-thirty. But the hours maintained in a country house, coupled with the travelling done by the guests that day and the recent excitement, had convinced all and sundry to retire early.

It was therefore in a quiet household that a select number of servants gathered in the old ballroom, which had been stripped of its picnic atmosphere. All traces of a certain chain of uncomfortable incidents had been removed, save in the minds of those gathered.

A small fire had been lit to chase away the chill of the evening, and several garden chairs were arranged near it. One chair was occupied by the copious form of Mrs. Formsby and across from her sat Tilbin, the butler. Closest to the fire was Nurse Rae, obviously still in great pain. Her splinted leg rested on a cushioned stool and was covered with a shawl.

Carlyle, a small, dapper man in a pince-nez, whose clothing proclaimed his station as a gentleman's gentleman, was just in the act of handing the nurse a cup of tea when Perkins the groom entered. He shivered and went to stand by the fire.

"Why are we meeting in this cavernous hole?" he demanded, holding his hands out to the blaze.

"The Room has been taken over by the visiting servants," Mrs. Formsby replied. "Besides those accompanying the general, Lord Edgemere and the Battentons, the Halstead people arrived tonight. I must say, such a bustle."

"Lord, don't I know it." Perkins turned to warm his backside. "We're put to it in the stables trying to find a place for all the cattle. Had to take his Grace's lamb and the ducks out of the stable."

"You didn't put the lamb back with the flock?" Carlyle asked, shocked.

"Don't be addlepated." Perkins turned to him. "Born out of season as he was, he'll have to be kept sheltered or he won't last the winter. The ducks, too. Dashed inconvenient, their arriving before their time—" He gave a crack of laughter. "Like the Halstead brat—begging the ladies' pardon."

Perkins was suddenly uncomfortable with his faux pas, and seeking a way out of it, he turned his attention to the earl's gentleman and then directed a censorious stare at Tilbin. "What's he doing here?"

The butler was not at all discomfited by the groom's disapproval. "Mr. Carlyle has earned his right to attend by taking it upon himself to protect Miss Portney at a considerable cost in dignity."

"How?" Perkins's frown denoted more curiosity than disapproval.

As head of the stables, and therefore an outside servant, Perkins was not a part of the household rank and not awed by even an earl's valet. But Carlyle's elevated position in the order behooved him to speak on a level that was, to Perkins, top-lofty in the highest degree.

The valet turned a cool stare on the groom.

"It takes no great amount of intelligence to understand your purpose. Furthermore I am an ally in spirit. Both for my lord's welfare and my own comfort, I also desire to see him happily wed." He paused for a moment in pleasurable contemplation of a settled existence. Then he remembered his explanation and brought himself back to the issue at the moment under discussion.

"When I saw Lord Battenton lying in wait for the young lady on whom I gather your hopes are at present placed, I made excuse to speak with him, preventing him from accosting her while she was alone. Since then the worthy Mr. Tilbin has been so kind as to apprise me of your efforts. I have volunteered to do what I can."

"I must inform you," Tilbin spoke up, "that Lord Battenton's attentions were too often directed towards Miss Amethy during luncheon."

"But how did Carlyle know?" Perkins demanded as a grin lit his face. "Don't tell me he was waiting table."

"Hardly," the valet answered. "However, being much in London, I do know the man's reputation. One and all are convinced the man is a, if the ladies will forgive me, a lecher—a creature of no discernible morals."

"Forgiven," Nurse Rae pronounced with decision, indignation at Lord Battenton swelling her thin chest.

"Most certainly." Mrs. Formsby physically enlarged her already ample bosom with indignation. "I will take care certain of my maids do not come into his presence. I am careful of the character of those in the household; they are innocent young females, if a bit flighty."

It was not surprising that Perkins, a handsome man with a rakish air, was forced to hide what would have been a most revealing grin.

The housekeeper continued. "I can not but wonder why the Battentons came here."

"Lack of funds on his part, and pinch-penny ways on hers," the valet answered promptly. "She's the dowager countess, the present earl's sister-in-law. She is comfortably fixed, but refuses to spend a shilling, and he hasn't one to his name. It's rumoured that he has hopes of controlling Miss Oglethorpe's fortune once she's reached her majority. She is, I believe, his niece."

"After she reaches her majority?" Tilbin looked surprised.

"After," Carlyle affirmed. "He is not the trustee of her father's estate, or it would have disappeared already."

"But why come here?" Perkins demanded. "He's too loose in the haft to be a friend of Northford—his lordship. For all our lord's rakehelly ways, he never runs sly."

"Lady Battenton is, I believe, a second cousin to Lady Susan," Tilbin informed Perkins. "Not the best branch of the family, that."

"Um-hmm," Perkins said, nodding, his curiosity satisfied. "There's talk from his coachman that his lord expects to be in high-pockets again before long—" Perkins hesitated as his attention fell on Nurse Rae. "Woman, with that broken leg, why aren't you abed, like a sensible person?"

"Because the situation demands that I be here," she returned with some asperity. "Everything we planned went completely amiss!"

"Oh, I don't see that at all," Tilbin leaned forward, his dignity for once overridden by his interest in the topic. "Notwithstanding the uproar, we are in a fortuitous position. Lady Halstead is confined for some time, and Lord Northford has insisted the entire family stay. There will be many opportunities for getting the couple together."

"If she stays," Nurse Rae cautioned, sounding morose. "You should know she most earnestly entreated her uncle to allow her to take the children and return to Halstead Manor."

"Any way to keep her from going?" Perkins asked.

"Lord Northford himself stopped it, though it was unintentional," the housekeeper continued. "He'd made a special point of saying he'd like the Halstead boys to stay as his Grace's guests. Lord Halstead didn't feel Miss Amethy could return alone.''

"If she stays, we can work out something," Perkins said, relaxing.

"Just having her here is not enough!" Nurse Rae snapped, her pain making her impatient. "The Halstead nurse has virtually abandoned her young gentlemen to be with her lady, and I am in no wise fit to see to the children—"

"So Mrs. Formsby will put one of her women in charge of the nursery," Perkins said shortly.

"It will not serve," Nurse Rae argued. "Not in the mind of Miss Portney, at least. Have you not noticed her concern for the children? She'll spend her entire time in the nursery."

"She was there all afternoon," Mrs. Formsby said, upholding the nurse's prophecy with irrefutable proof.

Perkins started to protest, but Tilbin raised an admonishing hand. "Our problem now is either to get her out of the playroom or my lord into it."

"That would be a sight worth seeing—the earl in the schoolroom," Perkins said, laughing.

"Harrumph. Those in the household may be fortunate enough to do so," Carlyle spoke thoughtfully. "My position affords me the opportunity to know something of my lord's mind. My lord has developed an affection for the child that is far above his responsibility, and indeed, he is coming to look upon the little fellow as his own."

"But even that won't get him into the schoolroom," Perkins argued.

"If my lord believed the child lost without his nurse and wished for his company, it just might suffice," Carlyle answered the groom's doubts.

"And of course, Mr. Carlyle would be the obvious one to drop a word in his ear," Tilbin said, sitting back in his chair, his formality quite forgotten as he smiled, contemplating the results.

CHAPTER FOUR

THE NEXT MORNING Amethy escaped to the nursery as soon as she could leave the breakfast parlour. While she was slightly ashamed of her feelings, she was a bit put out with her aunt for being the cause of her having to remain at Lowestroft. Her uncle had been correct; she could not return to Halstead Manor unchaperoned, nor was it proper for her to return home when her aunt had been confined. Still, having to remain in the residence of a gentleman who thought she was attempting to land him as a husband was exceedingly uncomfortable.

She had spent the previous afternoon and much of the evening in the nursery with the children, as much to avoid the earl's company as to be with them, and she was returning to them at that moment. He would see very little of her, she decided.

When Amethy entered the playroom, the three children seemed glad to see her and immediately plied her with questions concerning the arrival of Cedric Tooms.

"I didn't hear a carriage—he must have come very late," Jackie said as he nibbled his toast.

"I didn't even know I had a brother," Edward mused. "Why dothn't he live with uth, Amethy?"

"He will," she assured him, not quite sure how to answer their questions.

"He must be sick, because the doctor came to see him," Willy said as he concentrated on his porridge.

"Ate too many sugar biscuits," Jackie said. His explanation brought solemn nods from the Halstead children while Amethy stifled a smile and the nursery maids traded amused looks.

Willy found a book and brought it to Amethy.

"Will you read to us, Amethy?"

"Very well . . ." Seeing the look of disappointment on Jackie's face, she hesitated. "If that's what everyone wants. Jackie, what would you like to do?"

"You can read if you want to," he said, exhibiting a four-year-old's attempt at begrudged generosity.

"Perhaps you know of something more interesting to do," Amethy pursued. "What would you do if Nurse Rae were here?"

"Nurse Rae would take me to see Fluffy," he said, smiling hopefully up at her.

"I'd like that." Edward immediately cast his vote for the plan.

"Let's do," Willy said. "That's ever so much better than reading a book."

Amethy found no fault with the plan and had the maids bring jackets for the children. On the way to the stables, Jackie explained to the rest that he must visit the lamb every day, so it would know it was his. He gave his opinions on raising animals and animal husbandry in general. Willy and Edward accepted his theories, occasionally adding from their own experience of having two birds and a turtle. Amethy listened and tried to hide her smile. She wondered if Lord Northford had ever heard this philosophy.

But the happy conversation turned to heartbreak in the stable. The stall where the lamb and ewe were expected to be was inhabited by a carriage horse belonging to Lord Halstead.

"Fluffy's run away!" Jackie wailed.

"Most certainly not," Amethy spoke sharply, hoping to bring him out of his fears, but he was not to be persuaded too easily. At that moment a stableboy appeared, carrying a newly mended harness, and Jackie turned towards him.

"Holmes, where is my Fluffy?"

"Well, close my chaffer, your Grace..." The stableboy, upon seeing his Grace was accompanied by a lady, tugged his forelock and dropped his cant. "I'd not be knowing, your Grace, since Perkins—" to Amethy "—our head groom, had him moved to make room for the extra horses. On Lord Northford's orders, it was."

"Then tell Perkins we wish to see him immediately," Amethy demanded, hoping to forestall the tears she could see gathering in the child's eyes.

"But, mum, he's driven one of the gentry-morts—one of the ladies to the village." Holmes said.

"Very well, when he returns, ask him to step up to the playroom. We wish to visit the lamb this afternoon."

While waiting for the groom to return, Amethy tried to interest the children in playing with an elaborate set of carved soldiers. She was thus engaged when she heard shrill voices in the hall.

"Do see if you can arrange them better than I did," she requested of Edward, and as if a cold finger of caution prompted her, she paused at the doorway. Left alone they might set out in search of the lamb.

"And boys, I want your promise you will not come out into this passage," she said.

"I promise," Willy said, the grudging note in his voice proving her correct in her assumptions. Edward, too, seemed unhappy with her request, but Jackie agreed at once. As she closed the door, she thought she must watch her adventurous cousins, lest they lead the little duke into trouble. Her mind immediately turned to other matters as she heard Butts, her voice raised in indignation.

"I don't care if this is a duke's household, we don't do it that way at Halstead Manor!"

"Well, I can tell you, Mrs. Formsby will never allow—"

"My goodness!" Amethy threw up her hands in mock dismay. "Whatever can be the trouble?"

The maids, turning towards the doorway with blazing eyes, strove to improve their expressions before the young lady, but their faces were still sullen as they both pointed to a pair of trunks.

"Miss, trunks belong in the lumber room, not in a bedchamber," Maggie, the Lowestroft maid insisted.

"Not these." Butts, the Halstead nursery maid was determined to stand her ground. "Miss, these are full of the little gentlemen's favourite toys, and they must be at hand when wanted, else the entire household will suffer."

"And I am convinced that Maggie, who is doubtless a peer among nursery maids, will help you to solve your difficulty," Amethy said with a bright smile at the Lowestroft maid.

Her nobility appealed to, Maggie condescended to cooperate, and the maids were well on their way to a solution when Amethy hurried back to the playroom. She found her earlier fears justified. A quick look through the nursery apartments told her the children had somehow escaped on some adventure. She was crossing the room with the intention of ringing for the servants when a gust of wind, blowing in the open window, scattered ashes on the hearth.

As she crossed hurriedly to the window, no connexion between the window and the children crossed her mind, but as she reached out to catch the casement and pull it to, three scampering motions in the garden caught her eye. Even as she watched, unbelieving, Jackie led the way through a small opening in the hedgerow, and the little gentlemen of the Halstead family followed with no hesitation. All three boys disappeared into the woods beyond.

Amethy was surprised that they could have slipped out of the castle without being seen, but she was neither slow of wit, nor had she, as a child, been even slightly timid in her own escapades. She quickly grasped the meaning of the open window and the tree branch that came within inches of the wall.

"The little scamps," she gasped and threw the window wide. She was just raising both her skirt and one slipper-shod foot when she caught herself. For heaven's sake! She was no longer a six-year-old! It would doubtless bring her and all the Halstead family a high degree of embarrassment if she was caught climbing out the window, even in pursuit of the children.

Amethy was unfamiliar with the castle, so after reaching the ground floor, she wasted some minutes searching for a side door leading into the garden. Had she encountered a passing servant, she would have asked directions, but afraid her nephews had been the instigators of the escape from the nursery, she shrank from making an issue of the incident by calling for assistance.

More time lapsed, as having to use the front entrance, she was forced to wander through the garden on curving, mazelike paths until she discovered the opening in the hedge near the oak beneath the nursery window. Only after putting a rent in the flounce of her skirt and losing one of the tassels from her shawl did she manage to get through the narrow opening in the hedge. She was not in good humour when she started along the path through the thick copse, the only way the children could have taken.

More than an hour later, Amethy had been deserted by both her irritation and her assurance that she was on the trail of the boys. A number of paths led into the one she was using, but since they all seemed to be heading in the same general direction, she doubted the boys would have made a complete reversal of their course. Or would they?

Several times she paused, the third time she had decided to return to Lowestroft for help and had begun to retrace her steps when on the ground she espied a button and recognized it as being from Edward's coat.

Knowing now that she was on the path taken by the children, she turned and quickened her steps. Quite soon she came out of the wood. Topping a rise, she saw ahead of her the three little boys hurrying in her direction. Her relief at finding them was overweighed by the seemingly solid wall of ground fog creeping across the rolling meadow.

"Miss Amethy," Jackie cried out as he ran towards her. "We couldn't find Fluffy, and the mist is going to get us!"

Indeed, it seemed to Amethy that the mist was moving more rapidly than the children could walk.

"There are bad thingth in the fog!" Edward called, and his remark brought a wail of fear from Willy.

Amethy, unconcerned for her clothing, dropped to her knees as the children converged on her and gave each a reassuring hug.

"There is nothing in the mist but the field and the trees, even if they do look strange and fearful," she told Willy and Jackie.

They started back along the path with slightly more courage than Amethy had thought likely. Willy held one hand and walked slightly in front of her because of the narrow path, and Jackie gripped the other. Amethy appealed to Edward to bring up the rear because of his advanced age, and they again entered the wood, finding a problem almost immediately.

The narrow tracks leading into what Amethy thought of as the main path were indistinguishable from the one she had taken. Each appeared to be a fork and called for a decision. The arguments between Edward and Willy over the relative merits of each trail gave Amethy a throbbing headache. Jackie was content to follow Amethy and admitted to not knowing the way.

It seemed to Amethy that they had walked much farther than they should have when a tiny, dilapidated cottage seemed to grow out of the mist. It was immediately recognizable as an abandoned hovel, but at the side of the building a sagging roof projected out, held up by two flimsy-looking supports, which sheltered beneath it quite a sizeable amount of cut and stacked firewood.

"A little house," Willy announced the obvious.

"And firewood," Amethy added to his remark, thinking shelter and a fire would be a blessing. Not loath to admit to herself they were lost, she was willing to wait for rescue if they could be warm.

The one-room structure was devoid of furnishings, but on the slanting, uneven surface of the primitive mantel reposed a flint and rags. Leaving her shawl and reticule inside, Amethy led the boys outside to the neatly stacked wood.

"If we each take as much wood as we can carry, we'll soon have a nice cheery fire," she said. She hoped keeping them busy would calm their fears.

"I can carry some," Jackie said, his soft brown eyes doubtful, as if not at all sure, in spite of his willingness.

"I'm very strong and I can take heaps," Willy boasted.

"Not more than me!" Edward countered as he held out his arms. "Load me up and thee how much I can carry!"

Not really expecting the children to bring more than a piece or two, Amethy took an armload inside and returned for more. She was just rounding the corner of the building when Edward, so overburdened he could hardly walk, stumbled into the front post that formed half the roof support. The pole, only set upon the ground and held in place by the weight of the roof, slid outward.

"Careful!" Amethy cried and rushed to push it back in place. She determined to watch the children more carefully before some accident occurred.

By more luck than expertise, they soon had a bright fire in the cottage. The children were tired from their tramp through the woods and fell asleep on the floor. Amethy sat feeding the fire, wondering when the castle would be turned out to search for them.

The afternoon was quickly advancing. Amethy sat close to the fire, her shawl, which had protected her from the chill, now spread across the legs of the three children as they lay on the floor. The mist had now turned to rain and beat steadily upon the dirt path in front of the cottage. Some time later, it was with considerable relief that she heard the welcome sound of hoofbeats on the path. Rushing to the doorless entrance, she stood anxiously watching as Lord Northford came into sight, espied her, pulled his mount to a halt and quickly dismounted.

"Oh, my lord, you cannot imagine my delight in seeing you," she cried. "I was terrified lest we would not be found before morning. How I was to feed the children and keep them warm—"

"Then the boys are with you?" Relief tinged the earl's voice, but overriding that emotion was one of anger.

Amethy had not expected his attitude and stammered as she tried to explain. "Oh, y-yes, when I saw them slipping off—"

"You saw them leave the castle and you chose not to inform anyone?"

"At the time I saw no reason..." Amethy began her explanation before she examined her emotions, but when her temper flared over the injustice of his accusation, she stiffened. "I always attempt to aid and abet fugitives," she retorted.

He could believe what he chose, she decided. In his mood, the effort of convincing him was too great for the expected result. "And, my lord," she announced coldly, her hands balled into fists in her frustration, "if we are to continue this argument, I wish to do so out of the hearing of the sleeping children." Head held high and disregarding the rain, she marched regally through the door, around the side of the cottage and stepped under the shelter of the lean-to.

Lord Northford followed, his face still a mask of anger. Amethy was acutely aware of her dishevelled condition; the torn skirt, the cobweb only partially brushed from her sleeve. The stains of ashes and soot on both her clothing and her hands only served to reinforce her feeling of injury. The injustice became acute when the earl, after viewing her more closely, apparently found it necessary to control his quivering lips by rubbing a hand across his mouth.

Amethy repressed a most considerable desire to lash out at him and masterfully controlled her tongue as she invited, "Sir, since you are in no mood to accept an explanation, lay upon me any fault your temper may find applicable to the moment."

But Northford, continually a surprise to her, brought himself in check. Understanding appeared to take the place of his previous emotions.

"I begin to see your difficulty. You wished to protect the brats from punishment," he said, "but it does pass my comprehension that you did not return to Lowestroft."

Amethy stared at him aghast. "Sire, I am a stranger to the area, and since the children are not familiar with the wood, it would be conceivable to the weakest mind that we were lost!"

A slow smile lit Lord Northford's previously angry countenance.

As his humour grew and time passed with it, Amethy, worn by the afternoon's frustration, was brought to a considerably higher degree of agitation. She stamped one muddy slippered foot.

"Sir," she demanded, "I fail to see what you find so humorous in this situation."

Still smiling, Lord Northford raised one negligent hand and pointed over her shoulder.

Following the indicated direction, Amethy turned and beheld a sight that would have brought joy to her heart earlier in the afternoon, but at that moment filled her with consternation. She was gazing on the towers of Castle Lowestroft rising above the trees. The grey stone blended with the rainy afternoon, but it was clearly visible as it had not been when the fog held sway.

Amethy turned to face Northford and was ready to deliver a goodly piece of her mind when she saw the danger he was occasioning.

With the air of one who has thoroughly discomfited his opponent, he was leaning against the only sturdy support holding up the rude shelter that protected the firewood from the weather.

"Don't!" Amethy cried, but her warning came a shade too late.

Even the small amount of weight he placed against the post was sufficient to move it from its support. Immediately realizing his error, he struggled for his balance, but the smooth leather soles of his riding boots on the wet ground denied him secure footing for his balance. He was facing inwards, and his movements, as he tried to regain his footing, carried him farther beneath the shelter.

By the time he had regained his balance the damage was completely done. The post, old and insecure, had been dislodged and fell. The single support left, which had previously been rendered insecure when Edward stumbled against it, gave way. Amethy watched in horror while Northford struggled towards her. The old roof, attached only now to the building, dropped like the lid of a chest.

Amethy acted more from instinct than logic as she dropped to the ground in the open space between the stacks of cut wood.

Lord Northford was more resistant to their predicament and tried to remain standing. He took a severe blow to the head and shoulder and was knocked to the ground.

After the considerable noise of the splitting wood and the falling roof, silence prevailed. For a moment Amethy sat frozen by the calamity, unable to take it in. She was uninjured, having so precipitously flung herself down out of the way of danger. Across her outstretched legs she could feel the earl's arm, at first unmoving.

"M-m-my lord! My lord! Are you injured?" Her voice quavered. As she spoke, she felt his arm move slightly. Her eyes adjusted to the dimness, and she saw his head move; his arm was withdrawn.

There issued from him a cross between a moan and an oath. "Damn, I feel as if my shoulder was knocked off," he grunted.

He readjusted his position until he had moved up in close proximity to where Amethy could just barely sit upright, her hair brushing the underside of the now steeply slanting roof.

"Lord! What a mess," he grunted. "Of all the harebrained, hen-witted situations, this must be the worst."

Amethy decided her sympathy for him was unnecessary.

"My lord, if you have enough energy to condemn the situation, then may I suggest you do something to get us out of this ridiculous predicament?"

"Madam," he replied, his tones freezing, "if I correctly understand the situation, and I do not think a blow on the head has rendered me witless, I would not be here had you not brought us under this shelter for what I understood was to be an explanation of the afternoon."

The man was insufferable! "The explanation, my lord, is—if you had not insisted to my uncle that the children should remain at Lowestroft, I would have taken them back to Halstead Manor where we could have been comfortable."

"I see. I take it Lowestroft is not comfortable?"

"This, sir—" she waved her hand to indicate their present circumstances "—is hardly what I am accustomed to, nor do I usually end up at loggerheads with my host."

"Then I can only say, Miss Portney, that your hosts must struggle mightily to hold their tongues."

"That sir, is highly ungallant. I did not bring the roof down on us. And furthermore I find your total lack of chivalry amazing!"

The earl had been gingerly moving his injured shoulder, but he stopped and turned to gaze at her, his stillness showing his surprise. Then suddenly he threw back his head, his laughter echoing in the confined space.

"Chivalry, Miss Portney? My reputation hardly suggests a knight in shining armour."

Amethy, enraged as one is only when one's most secret dreams are discovered and made the object of humour, tossed her head and refused to look at him.

"I assure you, sir, you could never be confused with St. George!"

"At least I don't come home stinking of dragon smoke," he retorted.

"Nor, judging by your inactivity, are you a rescuer of maidens."

"Exactly what do you expect me to do?"

"I have no idea, but since your tales of prowess are often the on-dits of London, I suggest you do something."

The rain was easing off, but the day was still heavily overcast. Just enough light travelled through the chinks in the wood for Amethy to see the gentleman turn his head and then look away. He muttered something under his breath.

"I beg your pardon?" she said stiffly. "I did not understand you." When his answer was not forthcoming, she repeated herself.

"I said," he replied, his tone clear and crisp, "that there are some things you don't tell at card parties." There was in his admission such a little-boy reluctance that it chased from Amethy's mood all the irritation at her present position and she could not withhold a trill of laughter. Her mirth died away as she saw in his eyes a singularly enigmatic expression.

Then she heard three frightened little voices calling her name.

"And that's Thunder, Lord Northford's horse," Jackie shrilled in excitement. "Cousin Northford, where are you?"

Due to the enthusiasm in the children's voices, it took considerable volume from Lord Northford before his shouting drew the attention of the children. Then he was again perforced to raise his voice to its limits before they ceased their questions on how Amethy and Lord Northford could have been trapped beneath the roof.

Once the earl quieted their youthful rescuers, the question arose as to how they were to most expediently put to use the children's knowledge of where they were.

"If we are so close to the castle, would it not be better to send the children for help?"

"The paths twist about. They'd just get lost again."

Instead he worked out a plan for the children to remove some of the wood close to the building, in hopes of creating an opening large enough for Amethy and the earl to escape their entrapment.

Amethy objected to his plan. "You forget, they are children unused to the discipline of labour. You cannot use them as servants."

"They can handle it," he replied shortly.

Though displeased, she could think of no other way to better their condition, but when Jackie picked up a splinter in his hand and cried out in pain, she restated her fears.

"If any serious hurt occurs, the fault will be ours," she warned Northford. "I know my aunt would strongly disapprove."

Northford had been massaging his left shoulder and testing his arm. Twice he had braced himself and attempted, by the use of his uninjured shoulder and back to raise the roof, but either the amount of weight or his injury prevented him from having any success. While Amethy objected to the labours of the children he sat back and flipped open his snuff-box. With the expertise of long practice, he gracefully inhaled a pinch. The poise that had deserted him when the roof fell was back again.

"You're right, of course," he drawled. "And after some consideration, I wonder at my lack of gallantry."

Amethy thought it wonderful that he should notice his earlier manners and attempt to make amends, but she did think better of him for it...until he continued.

"Only a boor would be ungrateful for the opportunity to have a charming lady entirely to himself for the afternoon...if indeed we are rescued before nightfall. I doubt the servants will search through the night, even for us."

The idea of spending hours and possibly even the night trapped beneath the roof was enough to make Amethy shudder.

"And to tell the truth, with the number of guests at Lowestroft, this may be our only opportunity to enjoy a tête-à-tête." Though his eyes held a twinkle, clouds of meaning seemed to be moving just beyond their surface, causing Amethy to feel uneasy.

"Oh, no we're not," Amethy retorted. "This is certainly no social engagement."

"Ahh, but one must make use of one's opportunities," Northford replied tranquilly. "Perhaps I should thank the brats for their unwitting assistance." His brows were raised as he turned his head to observe the effect of his words on Amethy. "Perhaps I'd better instruct them to make our next entrapment more comfortable?"

"I wonder at your lack of instruction," she retorted. "I think it would have helped matters if you had familiarized the child with his own woods."

Northford gazed at her a moment before a smile escaped him. "And how do you suggest I do so? 'See here, brat, when you sneak out on your illicit adventures, use this path and not that one'—not quite appropriate for a four-year-old, do you think?"

"You need to do something!" Amethy loftily ignored the impracticality of her last suggestion.

"Then instruct me. But perhaps you had some more important purpose in mind when you brought us beneath this…" He waived a negligent hand towards the sharply canting roof.

Unable to sufficiently voice her feelings, she picked up a stick of firewood and tapped it against the stack, heartily wishing her position and training did not forbid her throwing it at him.

Northford held out his hand. "Give it to me. I'll start a pile here and take the rest from that stack," he said, pointing behind Amethy, where the sounds of the children working came from without.

Amethy's anger and a streak of perversity caused her to pause, then she placed the wood in his outstretched hand. A few splinters would be a small enough price to escape his company, and if she could create a tunnel to meet the one the children were starting, they would be released that much sooner.

They worked for some minutes in silence. Then from outside, Willy's voice rose plaintively.

"Cousin Amethy, can we stop now? I'm so tired."

"No!" Amethy was almost shouting. "Keep working! Get us out of here!"

"I'm tired too," Edward called.

"You promised to rescue me, now do it!"

Across the dimness, Northford was smiling. Amethy, tired, cramped from sitting on her feet and chilled to the bone, had nevertheless worked out her anger. Now she saw the purpose in the earl's remarks.

"You wanted to put me to work, too," she accused him.

He shrugged in answer. "Even with two good arms, I don't have the reach from there—" he indicated the stack from which Amethy removed the wood to the area where he was putting it "—to here."

"My lord, I see just how it was on your adventures. You were rescued from the geese by a band of travelling women and children. Hordes of them followed you around rescuing you from your scrapes, and you bought their silence with bonbons."

"And sugar biscuits," he retorted.

His idea to start from within, helping the children create an opening, appeared to be working quite excellently. He had, though gingerly, begun to use both arms when he paused, a length of firewood in each hand.

"Has my sight been affected by the blow, or is it getting dark? I'm having trouble locating empty spaces."

Amethy, who had been working diligently, paused, assessed what was in truth the deep twilight outside and hurriedly removed more wood, making a pile between herself and him.

"Don't speak so loudly, the children haven't noticed. I fear what will happen if darkness descends with them outside and us in here."

But Amethy was not long in learning, for several minutes later, Edward, who had been removing the wood from the pile and passing it to the other children gave out with a wail.

"Amethy, it'th getting dark," he cried out. "And the rain ith thtarting, too!"

The efforts from both sides of the wood pile had, by this time, created a small opening near the roof. Edward came through the opening and tumbled into Amethy's lap.

Before she could utter a protest, Willy, having seen his brother's action, called out to Jackie that they could get inside and immediately the other two children followed.

Neither Northford nor Amethy found it within themselves to voice a protest, but they understood the ramifications of the boys' actions. All attempts at clearing the firewood in order to clear a passage for escape would have to halt.

Jackie, the last one to climb in, sat in Amethy's lap. She could see in the dimness, his small face turned to hers.

"Miss Amethy, it's scary out there and it's cold in the rain," he said. His voice was so plaintive the only answer she could give was to put her arms around his small shoulders and hold him tightly.

"Well, that tears it," Northford grunted. "Now we're stuck here until someone finds us."

"Oh, if they only would," Amethy said plaintively.

"Don't be a goose," Northford snapped. "Of course they will. Thunder is still tied up outside."

Jackie gave a little sniffle. "We didn't find Fluffy," he said as he threw his guardian an accusing look. "You said I was to take care of him, but I can't find him. And by the time we get back, all the sugar cookies will be eaten up," he said.

"Buck up, brat. This is no time to behave like a baby," Northford chastised the child.

It was on Amethy's lips to ask him how he could expect a four-year-old to behave like an adult, when with surprising understanding he added, "And if the sugar biscuits are all gone, there will still be tarts."

And quite obviously, Northford did have a particular understanding of his ward's nature. A small arm encircled Amethy's neck, and Jackie whispered into her ear.

"I like tarts, too."

"My favourites," Amethy said, and would have added more had not Northford interrupted.

"I do not think a long dissertation on F-O-O-D is wise," he reminded her.

She was inclined to agree. Hunger pangs were bothering her, as well. It was in her mind to try to avert the attention of the boys from their present predicament, but hunger and discomfort from their position and the chill of the evening seemed to be fogging her mind.

Northford, too, was quiet and the children were silent. After their labours and discomfort in the darkness, they seemed to be well satisfied for a few minutes just to be in the company of adults.

They had just begun to stir restlessly and renew their complaints when the welcome sound of horses' hooves coming down the path announced the arrival of others on the scene.

"Hallo! Here's Northford's horse," called out Lord Halstead.

At the sound of their father's voice, both of the Halstead children set up a clamour. From without came the confusion of horses being brought to a halt, a shouting of questions, and neighing cattle, and the sound of footsteps breaking damp twigs. Identifiable by their voices were Lord Halstead, Viscount Edgemere, Perkins the head groom, and Holmes the stableboy.

From within the confines of the shelter, Amethy, Lord Northford and all three children tried to answer the questions at one time. To halt the ensuing confusion required a shout from Lord Northford so strong in volume that Amethy must cover her ears.

But after a hurried though low conversation, the gentlemen on the outside concocted the simplest and most speedy plan for releasing those trapped under the roof.

With an expediency Amethy could only admire, the four of them, with a mighty heave, raised the lower portion of the roof sufficiently so that the five underneath could scramble out.

By the light of lanterns, brought by Holmes and Perkins, Amethy was able to judge the degree of her own dishevellment by viewing that of Lord Northford and the children. Their clothes were dirty, wrinkled, their hair was askew, and she knew that no better condition served to present her.

She brushed ineffectively at her clothes and ran fingers through her short curls. The children who had clung to her so tightly that afternoon abandoned her for others from whom they sought comfort. Willy and Edward were placing grimy little hands around their father's waist.

"Cousin Amethy got us lost," Willy told his father.

The little duke, apparently having had a surfeit of both Amethy and Lord Northford's company, had thrown himself into the arms of Perkins, the head groom.

"I couldn't find Fluffy," he sobbed, giving his explanation again for the third time.

After all the questions were answered, the children and Amethy were set in the saddles while the men led their mounts on the short distance to the castle. Lord Northford brought up the end of the line with Amethy sitting sideways on his saddle, one stirrup shortened for her.

"I really wish you had ridden, my lord," Amethy enjoined him for the third time since they'd begun the journey to the castle. If she didn't cease her complaints she would become another Lady Battenton, she decided, but as the earl walked in front, leading Thunder, he occasionally twisted his torso as if searching for some ease of pain.

"I need to walk," he had replied twice, but the third time he answered her he was not so mannerly.

"Miss Portney, is it necessary that you wrap all nobility in cotton wool? I assure you I am as capable of using my legs as is Holmes or Perkins. As able to do so as the children were capable of removing the wood and securing our freedom—had they chosen to do so."

"Then, sir, please do walk if you are that determined to do so! But I will tell you to your head that I find your remarks totally out of order and without one whit of justification."

"I beg your pardon."

"I would have said as much, had Holmes or Perry been leading—"

"Perkins."

"Had Perkins been leading the horse with an injured shoulder," Amethy continued as if the correction were commonplace. "Furthermore, the children could have been hurt, being so young and unused to the task. And while I'm on the subject of danger, you must do something about that tree—or at least the limb that approaches the nursery room window."

"I will not cut down that tree!" Northford's anger gave Amethy cause to think the subject had been raised before.

"My lord, that limb presents a danger to his Grace," Amethy argued, using formality in hope of pointing out to him that being guardian of a duke was no light charge.

"Left to you women, his Grace is all he'll ever be," Northford retorted. "I don't care what title he holds, he's still a boy. When you were a child, didn't you ever climb a tree?"

"I wasn't a duke."

"Your father's a viscount?"

"He is," Amethy answered, wondering where this turn of the conversation was leading. Her attention was so devoted to the argument that she entirely missed seeing a low branch until it was directly in front of her. She ducked quickly, and in her efforts to avoid the branch, she lost her balance. Her squeak of alarm brought Northford around the horse in time to catch her in his right arm, thereby preventing her from losing her balance as she slid from the saddle.

For a moment he held her, but the cloudy night kept his expression hidden from her.

"The Honourable Miss Amethy Portney," he murmured, when she had regained her balance. His lips came down on hers, soft but urgent. His kiss drove away the chill and the dampness of the night. She was inundated with the thrill of an excitement she had never imagincd possible.

Then he stepped back, leaving her gazing at him with wide-eyed astonishment.

"The Honourable Miss Amethy Portney," he repeated, "but despite her birth, once a child and now a woman."

He turned away and led the horse down the narrow track, leaving her staring after him until common sense overtook surprise and outrage. She hurried to follow before she was lost in the darkness.

CHAPTER FIVE

AMETHY, AWAKENED quite late the next morning, puzzled over the remark from Carrie, her maid, until a Lowestroft maid entered the bedroom carrying a heavily laden breakfast tray.

"She's a sensible country-bred woman who doesn't coddle them that's not sick, but he insisted."

The she was apparently Lady Susan, which made the he Lord Northford.

"How considerate," Amethy replied, hastily arranging herself to accept the tray across her knees.

"Considerate! A little late I should think—a good dress ruined. Those slippers worn only twice...."

Carrie's complaints went unheard as full memory of the previous afternoon came back to Amethy. She remembered it with a lack of reality, a kaleidoscope of fear, anger and tender feelings, their varying colours all tumbled together in an emotional upheaval.

Remembering she was thinking of Northford, a man of infamous reputation who had the gallantry of a cart horse, she attempted to push away her softer feelings and concentrated on the last outrage of the evening. How could he have been so callous as to take advantage of her slipping from the saddle to kiss her when she was off balance? Then he walked off and left her standing in the dark on a strange path in the woods!

Her lips curved in a smile. Had it been daylight, she would have been able to see only the length of the horse separated her from the gate through the hedge. The smile disappeared. He could have told her that!

Afterwards, her desire to deliver to him a considerable piece of her mind was thwarted by the little duke, who, despite his fear of the dark shadows in the garden, had waited for her and put his small trusting hand in hers. Unable to rip up at his guardian with the child present, Amethy was forced to hold her tongue as the three of them traversed the passages through the castle and came upon the main stairway just as Lady Battenton and Miss Oglethorpe stepped out of the drawing room.

Lady Battenton's protruding eyes took in the dishevelled condition of the three just getting ready to ascend the stair. Her censure was blatant.

"I daresay Ruth is quite shocked. I'm sure she will wish to know if what we see is to be the style of dress for dinner this evening?"

"Oh, Aunt Elvira, I'm sure..." Miss Oglethorpe, quite as embarrassed as Amethy, appeared to lack the words to finish her objection.

Amethy, exquisitely sensible of her appearance, was most desirous of sinking through the floor, and her discomfiture was considerably heightened when the earl turned a long, appraising gaze upon her.

"For my part," he drawled, turning back to Lady Battenton after his scrutiny of Amethy, "I would be delighted to lead Miss Portney into any company—as she is, or in any guise she might choose—and I assure you, Elvira, she would set the fashion." He gave Amethy the deepest of bows and, taking her arm, led her up the stairs.

Behind them, Lady Battenton expostulated to Miss Oglethorpe, who ineffectually tried to reason with the outraged woman.

When they were out of hearing, Amethy's eyes twinkled as she smiled up at the earl, all her discomfort melted in the warmth of his approval.

"My lord, you are unconscionable," she said, laughing.

When they reached the first floor, Northford sent the little duke to the nursery with a footman. Then he took Amethy's arm and walked with her towards her apartment. "I feel I must offer you a word of caution."

Amethy, thinking he was referring to the recent escapade, looked up with fire in her eyes. "Sir, I realize now the rashness of my actions, and I can assure you it will not happen again."

A slow and most tantalizing smile crossed Northford's face. "My dear Miss Amethy," he said, "rashness is becoming a way of life when trying to keep up with that brat I manage. That's not my concern. The warning I feel you should heed is to not allow yourself to be alone with Lord Battenton."

Amethy was stunned. Was he accusing her of being a flirt? Did he think she would seek the gentleman's company? She drew herself up, and her amethyst eyes flashed. Her words were clear. "Sir, I have not sought that gentleman's company nor do I think he will seek mine, so I am sure your warning is quite unnecessary." She would have turned away, but just at that moment he caught her hand.

"My dear young lady," he said, his voice, though cool, was soft, "any gentleman with an eye for beauty and the desire for charming company would most certainly seek you out. I'm sure that in your seasons in London you were warned to eschew the company of a number of gentlemen. I suggest you watch this one." With that, he raised her fingers to his lips and the kiss that he placed upon them was so lingering and his eyes upon her face so soft that when he gave her another elaborate bow and stepped back, Amethy found herself somewhat breathless.

Not knowing how to handle the situation, she immediately turned on one muddied heel and fled to her apartment.

So deeply had Northford's attentions affected her that at dinner she found it difficult to raise her eyes from her plate. When good manners made it imperative that she take part in the conversation, she found his gaze resting upon her face. He appeared to be speculating about her as though she were somehow different than he had at first supposed, and his gaze occasioned a recurrence of all her confusion.

Telling herself she was behaving like a silly chit not yet out of the schoolroom, she had pleaded fatigue after the adventure and hurried to her room, determined to bring her emotions under control.

And she had done so, she told herself as she called Carrie to take away the breakfast tray. She spent most of the evening reminding herself of Northford's reputation. She would continue to remember it.

By Northford's orders, the children had been put to work at lessons that morning to keep them from mischief. Her aunt was too occupied with young Cedric to be bothered with a mere niece, so Amethy decided to take advantage of the nice day and take her needlework into the garden.

She had reached the foot of the stairs in the main entrance hall when General Duckworth, Lords Battenton and Edgemere, and Lady Susan stepped out of the gallery. By their dress, the lady, the general and the viscount were prepared for a ride, an opinion reinforced by the opening of the front doors by a footman allowing Amethy to see, just outside, three horses saddled and ready.

"I say there, Miss Portney, good day for a ride," General Duckworth called across the hall. "Delighted to wait if you wish to go with us."

Amethy smiled and shook her head. "Not for the world," she said, laughing. "You would not under any circumstances wish me along if you knew of my ability on a horse." With a wave of her hand, she turned towards the side hall that would take her into the garden. She had just seated herself on one of the benches when, from somewhere hidden from her vision, rose a contretemps. A scuffling sound and a fall was almost immediately followed by swearing and she recognized Lord Battenton's voice. Some poor servant was receiving a most vociferous censure, and Amethy was on the point of rising to see what the problem might be when almost immediately the argument was halted and quick footsteps receded.

Knowing there was nothing she could do at that point, she pulled out the length of silk with which she intended to continue her embroidery and discovered her needles were missing. She gave an exclamation of annoyance and determined to return to her room to see if by some accident she had removed them from the basket.

Her walk became longer than she expected. At one turning she stepped between the hedges expecting to

find a throughway and came upon another recess in
which sat Miss Ruth Oglethorpe. At first glance, that
young lady, too, appeared to be simply enjoying the
sun of a warm afternoon while busy plying her needle
hemming a linen handkerchief. But in seeing movement at the entrance of the sheltered area, she looked
up and in her dark eyes was hope and expectancy that
died to disappointment.

Not wishing to be on the scene for what she knew
must be a planned secret meeting, Amethy made more
of her irritation over her mistaken path than was totally necessary.

"I declare," she said, with a deliberate and obvious frown, "I will never find my way through these
most confusing hedges."

"Indeed, they do get a person tangled about in the
head," agreed Miss Oglethorpe. Then noticing Amethy's basket, she nodded at it quite pointedly. "Are
you, too, enjoying the warm morning with a little
sewing?"

"That was my expectation," Amethy answered.
"Unfortunately I find I have left my needles above
stairs. I'm just on my way to retrieve them now."
That, she thought, would give her an excuse for making an immediate leave-taking, certain the young
woman would be relieved to be left alone again. So she
was surprised when Ruth detained her.

"There's no need," she said, searching in the bag
that held her own sewing supplies. "Use one of mine.
It would be ever so much nicer to have someone to talk
with while we sew."

Amethy stood for a moment, her indecision not allowing her to speak. Certainly she could not have been
so wrong about Miss Oglethorpe or what she had seen

in her eyes. The disappointment had been evident. So why, thought Amethy, would the young lady be willing to share her company if she was momentarily expecting someone she wished to meet in secret?

Her invitation had sounded quite genuine, and Amethy sensed the young woman was making an effort to overcome her painful shyness. Her face, too, had undergone a change, both hope and disappointment had faded and in its place came a slight look of wistfulness that Amethy could neither be sure she saw nor quite ignore.

Though Ruth was much of an age with Amethy, she seemed younger and more vulnerable.

Amethy accepted the needle, sat down and began stitching. For some minutes they sat working in a silent companionship that seemed to add energy to each one's work, and yet they found very little to say.

Several voices drifted across the garden; the housekeeper was taking advantage of the unseasonably warm day to open the windows and air the rooms.

Almost without thought, Amethy looked up the side of the castle, her eye finding the nursery window. Framed in it she saw the three small faces of the children and waved, smiling as they waved back.

Miss Oglethorpe's gaze had followed hers and a small chuckle escaped the young lady. "Perhaps I should not speak of it," she said, shyly, "for I'm sure it was a most uncomfortable situation, but I must admit to being greatly diverted by the tale I have heard of the children's escapade."

Amethy nodded, giving a slight smile to take the sting from her words. "I, too, may find the situation humorous five years from now, but nothing is less comfortable than being trapped under a roof, in a woodpile, in the dark. I was in exquisite terror that some small creature would come crawling out from beneath the wood and go skittering across my lap."

Miss Oglethorpe's eyes widened. "I confess I had not considered that possibility."

"You would have, had you been in my place," Amethy replied. "I am persuaded their speedy lifting of that roof to allow our escape was all that kept me from dissolving into hysterics at any moment."

The young lady's cheeks took on a brighter tinge. "Did Robert—did Lord Edgemere assist in raising the roof?" she asked.

Amethy noticed the young woman's sudden high colour, which gave her face life and beauty. She searched her mind for some way to give the young lord a bit of heroism in the story. "I am persuaded they could not have done it without him," she said. "I must believe it was a great deal due to his strength that we were accorded such a speedy rescue."

The gratified expression on Ruth's face removed any doubt that it was indeed Lord Edgemere that she had been awaiting.

"I believe his heroism has won him an invitation to join Lady Susan and General Duckworth on a much-touted ride," Amethy volunteered in an attempt to give Ruth an explanation of why the viscount had not kept the tryst and to do so without letting Miss Oglethorpe know Amethy knew her secret.

But Ruth received the news with equanimity. She nodded, keeping her eyes on her sewing for a moment and then looked up, her gaze most candid. "I thought some such had happened," she said. After a pause she went on, "I fear I'm not successful as a dissembler. I'm sure you knew I was waiting for someone."

Not knowing what to say, Amethy nodded.

As though she had opened the gate in the spillway of a dam and then was powerless to close it against the rush of water, Ruth Oglethorpe began to explain. "I'm sure my behaviour must seem quite wanton," she said.

Amethy stopped her, not wishing to be rude, yet the tediousness of the explanation and the discomfort it would bring would serve no purpose. "I cannot think it wanton for old friends to meet," she said calmly.

Amethy's answer did nothing to calm the young lady; after one terrified look she dropped her eyes to her sewing and stitched with trembling fingers.

Amethy continued to ply her needle. She had heard and ignored the gossip of the servants, but Ruth's fear gave veracity to the tale that she was under the thumb of her uncle. According to Amethy's maid, the strict trustees of the young lady's fortune prevented Lord Battenton from using it for his own debts, but Ruth would shortly reach her majority when she would control her own wealth. The earl would then be able to browbeat her into doing as he saw fit.

All Carrie's dark prophecies had not moved Amethy as much as that look of fear on Miss Oglethorpe's face. Her heart went out to the young woman in her plight.

"I do think Lord Edgemere would have been here if he could," Amethy said.

Ruth nodded, not raising her eyes from her sewing. "Yes, I had so hoped...." Her fleeting glance met Amethy's. "He went to my father two years ago, but then he was without expectation. Now that he's ascended to his uncle's honours and fortune..."

Amethy could think of few reasons why Ruth found the subject too painful to proceed. Her immediate thought was the young lady's doubts about Lord Edgemere's continued affection.

"I doubt his affections have altered, since he is here because of your visit."

"Would I could think so," Ruth replied, "but in truth, Lady Susan and General Duckworth are friends from their youth. Robert was not expecting to meet me here."

"His delight in seeing you would auger well for his continued feelings." Amethy offered what solace she could. "You hope his feeling is still the same," she prompted when Ruth did not continue.

Ruth nodded, her shoulders sagging. "But what use? Though I reach my majority in four days, I am still trapped by circumstances."

Amethy could think of nothing to say.

They sat sewing in a companionable silence for a few minutes before they were interrupted by a footman who came to announce luncheon was being served in the dining room. They made haste to pack up their sewing and hurried to the dining room, but they were the last to arrive at the table. And though Amethy might deplore much of the insensitivity for others that Lady Battenton exhibited in her selfishness, she could not but be glad that the woman was so busy with her complaints that she had taken everyone's attention away from their late arrival.

Amethy took her place with a sigh, and only after she was seated did she notice the strong lines of disapproval in both Lord Northford's and Lord Halstead's expressions. That drew her attention most forcefully to the subject of the lady's complaints.

"And I do think if one does not feel sufficiently well to traverse the distance between the dining room and the apartments I have been assigned, which I do feel are quite unnecessarily far removed considering my condition..."

Amethy's mind quickly reviewed the layout of the passage in the guest wing of the castle and the apartments thus opening on to it. The Halstead party, because of Lady Halstead's confinement, had indeed been given the preference of nearness to the public rooms. Around the table, other eyes turned inward, all making the same review and arriving at the same conclusion.

Oblivious to the disapproval of the others, Lady Battenton changed the subject of her complaint. "And I cannot understand what so many people find to do in the country," she went on, her voice rising in a whine. "At least I think we could have some civilized activities. Miss Portney, you and Ruth and I will play whist this afternoon."

Amethy's mouth fell open in what she knew must be a most unbecoming manner. Before she could voice either acceptance or the excuse her mind was frantically seeking, Lady Susan, who gave the appearance of never hearing anything that occurred, suddenly spoke up.

"I have asked Miss Oglethorpe to ride into the village with me," she said promptly.

Amethy looked across the table at the young lady and saw her attempt to hide her surprise. But unexpected plans seemed to be in the air. Lord Northford, who had remained tight-lipped and silent through Lady Battenton's complaints, suddenly had an announcement of his own.

"Miss Portney is engaged to ride out with me," he said shortly. "I require assistance controlling those brats, and I'll not be bothered with the twitterings of a maid."

Amethy ducked her head and pretended interest in her plate as she gave an affirmative nod. She chastised her racing pulse, reminding herself he was Northford, after all, and not to put any unjustified meanings on his invitation. Building her defence, she tried to tell herself he was high-handed and should have consulted her before making plans. Her objections died stillborn; the children would be out of the nursery, all three boys would find it a particular treat to be in his company and she had been rescued from Lady Battenton.

Since the cloud bank in the west portended the possibility of cooler weather in the afternoon, Amethy returned to her room for a cape. As she descended the main stairway into the entrance hall, only a few paces in front of her she saw Maggie, the nursery maid descending the steps with the three children.

They ran immediately to Northford full of questions as to where they were going.

"Quiet, brats, or back to the nursery." he announced, pulling on his gloves.

Amethy, reaching the floor and approaching them, said, "I beg pardon, sir, but will I, too, be returned to the playroom if I ask questions?"

"Most certainly not," Northford answered, a glint in his eye. "Your..." He paused in an attempt to hold his mouth straight. The crinkles around his eyes gave him away. "Your success in that direction is not what one would call phenomenal."

"My lord, I think I do better in the nursery than you do with a roof," Amethy replied. Straightening her hat, she swept out of the door in front of him.

Seeing nothing amiss with the arrangements, Amethy walked down the three shallow steps to the courtyard and approached the farm cart that was hitched to an elderly and spiritless horse. Behind the cart, the magnificent Thunder was standing saddled, bridled and led by a groom.

The children, once freed from the maid, raced down the steps and climbed into the cart, calling to Amethy to join them. Only Northford stood in the doorway obviously displeased with some arrangement.

"Holmes," he demanded of the young man holding the horse. "Why did you bring Thunder? And why is that animal harnessed to this cart? I distinctly said I wanted Jason between the shafts."

Holmes fingered the reins nervously. "That prime 'un took one look at that cart and threatened to kick the floorboards in should we try to force him between the shafts."

"Are you saying he considered himself too good to pull this cart?" Lord Northford frowned at the groom who grinned up at him.

"If I was you, my lord, I don't think as how I'd be too anxious to let that bit of blood see me driving this cart. He might not handle right from then on. That's how come me 'n Perkins thought maybe you'd care to ride, seeing as how I could drive the cart."

Northford's irritation gave way to a grin.

"It comes to something when my horse is a bigger snob than I am," he said with a smile, as he walked down the steps and approached the cart. "I'll drive this bag of bones."

"Uh...my lord—"

Amethy could hardly censure the earl for the frown that creased his features. He had accepted the change in his plans with an equanimity she thought wonderful. Now to have the groom argue with him was a little much.

"What's wrong now?" Northford snapped.

"Well, Old Turtle here has got some funny ways...." The groom paused as if in some confusion as to how to explain what he wanted to say.

Northford turned haughty. "Are you saying I can't drive this beast?"

"He's a tricky one."

Northford appeared slightly bored. "I've never seen an animal I couldn't manage, and I won't start with this wolf bait!" With that he climbed into the back of the farm cart, bodily rearranged the children by putting them where he wished them to be and offered Amethy his hand.

Try as she might, she couldn't keep the laughter from her eyes as she stepped up into the cart and took her seat. "Do have a care with this creature, my lord. I would not wish to find myself trapped under an overturned cart after yesterday's experience."

"That will be enough out of you," Northford said shortly, favouring her with a half-amused glance as he took the reins and gave the animal the signal to start.

"Oh, Cousin Northford wouldn't turn over the cart," Jackie told her, patting her hand in case she was worried. "He's a real out-and-outer!"

This bit of information brought Northford's head around as he critically eyed the child who sat immediately behind him. "Where did you get that term, brat?"

"I…umm…" Jackie looked about wildly as if some idea lay in the bottom of the cart. "I must have heard it somewhere," he said.

Northford's head immediately snapped forward. Amethy, also somewhat forward of the children in the cart, glanced over and saw his jaws working and the crease deepening and lessening in his cheeks as he tried to keep away his laugh.

"Methinks 'twould be better to lock this rapscallion in the tower until he's passed his salad days," Northford muttered.

Amethy scrambled for her handkerchief to cover her mouth, stifling a laugh. But she did feel the earl could be a bit more careful about the company the child was allowed to keep. She could certainly not see that type of remark coming from either Edward or Willy and so was a bit shocked when Willy nodded sagely.

"Drives to an inch, I daresay."

While Amethy choked in surprise, Northford developed a sudden fit of coughing. He had been paying strict attention to his driving, holding the ribbons quite properly in both hands, but in order to be mannerly in his attempt to hide his laugh, he had switched the reins to his right hand. That movement was sufficient to give Old Turtle his opportunity.

He immediately veered off to the left, causing the cart to lurch in the farm-road rut, and it appeared for some moments that Amethy's warning to Lord Northford was about to become a prophecy. On each side of the road, ditches some three feet deep made an abrupt edging to the travelled way. The cartwheel below her was only inches from sliding into the ditch when the earl gained full control of the ribbons and jerked the old horse back in line.

"Here, you devil! You're not messing with some farm boy!" Northford snarled.

Amethy had been quite frightened for a moment, but she recovered quickly. "I daresay he realizes that," she said with a smile. "I did take it from the stable-boy's warning that those who are used to driving him know to watch for his tricks."

"I was watching," Northford asserted. "And he knew exactly what he was doing."

Turtle's ears twitched as if he were listening. Amethy agreed with Northford, but she chose to give the incident another meaning.

"Can it be, my lord," she asked thoughtfully, "that in those daring exploits of horsemanship that I heard so much of in London, there were also incidents you did not tell at card parties?"

Northford threw her a darkling look. "I knew I'd regret that admission," he said.

Behind them the three children were busy chattering about every animal, fence post and tree they passed when Northford turned the cart onto an even smaller farm track and in a few minutes brought it to a halt in front of a cottage and some outbuildings.

A boy of about twelve came out of a stable and rushed forward to take Turtle's ribbons. He pulled his forelock out of respect for Lord Northford, but didn't speak.

The earl ushered the boys out of the cart, offered Amethy his hand and, to her surprise, led the four of them to the stable. In a well-kept stall inside, Amethy, who was in front of the children, saw the ewe and the baby lamb that had been in the ballroom at Lowestroft. The little duke, as he looked around, gave a squeal of delight and ran forward.

"Fluffy!" he shouted. "Cousin Northford, look! It's Fluffy."

Northford raised his eyebrows in mock surprise. "Dear me, I wonder what he's doing here."

Amethy's skirts were brushed as Edward and Willy raced around her, their squeals of glee as loud as the little duke's. She and the earl stood watching a moment as the boys petted the lamb and then Northford took her arm, leading her out of the stable.

Amethy smiled fondly at him despite her desire to keep the banter going. "I am to judge from this, sir, that you did not heartlessly turn the animal out to a cold winter where he'd most certainly perish?"

"You wrong me, madam," Lord Northford replied. "Certainly I would have turned him out to freeze in the snow. Apparently something went wrong with my instructions."

They had been walking slowly towards a rough-hewn bench placed beneath the shade of an ancient chestnut. As they reached it, Lord Northford offered Amethy a seat.

"Sorry, no better accommodations. There's just old Hawkins and his grandson here." He looked about. "Hawkins must be out in the fields."

"But who takes care of them?" Amethy looked around at the well-kept farmyard. The stable had beer clean and the boy reasonably so.

"A typically female remark," Northford replied, flipping open his snuff-box. "Why is a woman never capable of believing that men can exist without them?"

Suddenly there was in Amethy an added meaning in her remark that grew out of her *tendre* for the earl. Irrationally feeling he had interpreted her emotions, she dissolved into acute embarrassment and reacted much more strongly than she intended.

"That, sir, is the ungallant remark of a man who can very easily overlook the care of his aunt, a household full of maids and Mrs. Ponsby!"

"Mrs. Formsby," Northford corrected her as he leaned against the tree that shaded the bench. His slow, crooked smile invited indignation, and Amethy was more than willing to accommodate him.

"I'm surprised you even know her name," she snapped, her dark mood increased by her slip and his amusement.

"Ahh, but I always know the names of the females in my life," he said softly, his eyes on hers. "I know their names, their moods..." He straightened up from his leaning position and came forward to sit on the end of the bench. "I know the colour of their eyes—the way they flash in anger and soften in affection..." His gaze travelled over her face, an explorer hungry for knowledge of new terrain.

The clouds of thought were moving just under the surface of his eyes again. Amethy, caught up in the charm of his words, stared into those grey depths, seeking to know the meaning and hoping what she found fit her feelings.

His gaze lingered on her left cheek like a warming touch, bringing sensation to her skin until she could feel unbidden movement at the side of her mouth. He was making love to her! Or was he? Amethy's strict upbringing demanded she put him in his place, but how, she could not fathom, for not one word had actually referred to her.

His eyes moved ever so slightly. "I know the beauty of their small, pointed chins, those rose petal cheeks and their lips that turn up in sweet smiles...."

Amethy sat breathless, caught in the magical web he was weaving, but good sense intruded and she struggled to regain her composure. She refused to let him know how he was affecting her.

"I'm sure no female escapes your notice," she retorted, her voice crisp.

His eyes filled with laughter. "I acknowledge a hit, ma'am. But tell me, are you sure your gallant knight, the personification of St. George would be any better?"

There Amethy felt on safe ground.

"This mythical gentleman you keep referring to would be above such things," she answered, her smile accepting the victory of another verbal thrust, but she was too early in claiming her win.

"If I remember correctly, St. George was known for rescuing damsels. That fellow probably had a house full of strange women. How would you like a man who brought home every chit he found?"

"Oh, you're impossible!"

Frustration brought Amethy to her feet. "I must see to the children," she gasped, and hurried towards the barn. What could be the man's design, she asked herself, and attempted to answer with the obvious. He was a rake, a libertine, and she must keep his past in mind, but when she was with him, she seemed to forget everything she knew.

She hurried to the stall where the children generously allowed her to pet Fluffy, but while she absently stroked the small woolly head, her mind stayed on the man who had remained in the farmyard.

On the return trip, Northford proved that his tolerance for his ward's antics didn't preclude an occasional order.

"There'll be no more trips looking for the lamb," Northford was saying to Jackie as he drove the farm cart back towards Lowestroft. "Fluffy will remain at High Farm until we have room for him in the stables again."

Before leaving the castle Amethy had had the foresight to send Carrie to the kitchen for three large sugar biscuits, which she had wrapped in a napkin and tucked in her reticule. Since Willy and Edward were showing signs of tiring and coming close to an argument, she searched out the treats and handed one to each of the children.

"Sugar biscuits," Jackie said, his eyes lighting up. Remembering his manners, he offered a portion to Amethy and when she refused, broke off a sliver and gave it to his cousin.

"Generous of you, brat," Northford said, noticing the small portion he had been given and making a show of nibbling at it.

Again he had transferred the ribbons to one hand, the experience they had had on the way to the farm now forgotten.

With the presence of mind not indicated by his drooping head and ears, Turtle immediately turned to the right. Before Northford could get the reins sorted out again, they felt a sickening lurch as the right wheel of the farm cart slid off into the deep ditch. The horse's triumphant whinny joined Northford's oath, the squeals of the children and Amethy's cry as they tumbled to the right side of the cart and ended in a soft but tangled landing against the muddy bank.

Northford's blue superfine coat of exquisite London tailoring was muddied down one side and on the back. Amethy, who had fallen partly across him, had been wearing her cape only lightly draped over her shoulder. It had fallen partly to the side, so the shoulder of her dress, its short sleeve, her arm and part of her cape showed the telltale signs of mud and the blue brim of her bonnet had a brown border at the edge of her vision. All three children showed the stains of the accident.

Edward, tired and disliking obvious dirt, gave Northford an accusing look. "I thought you were thuppothed to be a whip!" he announced.

Northford stared down at the child and then looked over at Amethy. "There are days, and then there are days," he said quietly.

While Amethy ineffectually attempted to brush the mud from her clothing and that of the children, Northford unharnessed the horse, promising the old animal a series of horrible fates. Northford's prophecies about the animal's fate were impossible to achieve all at once or even in any conceivable order.

Once the animal was freed from the shafts, they began their trek towards Lowestroft. Amethy lifted her skirts and looked ruefully at her green kid boots. They were the second pair of shoes in two days to be completely ruined.

The children walked ahead; Northford led the horse and accompanied Amethy. His jaws were set in determination.

"I am going to kill this animal."

Amethy looked up at him with no trace of humour in her blue-violet eyes. "My lord, being gently raised, I shrink from both bloodshed and violence. However, in this particular case, should you be generous enough to allow it, I would take it as a favour if I were able to assist you."

"Madam—" his brows raised slightly "—do I detect a hint of savagery in your dimpled nature?"

"Alas, you do," she replied quietly. "For have you thought ahead? I do not believe fortune will allow me to gain the seclusion of my room and change my clothing without coming under the gaze of Lady Battenton. I shudder to think what she will have to say."

He nodded solemnly and offered her his arm as they came to a series of ruts that made walking difficult. To Amethy it seemed both surprising and comforting that they could be in such accord.

WHEN CARLYLE, the Earl of Northford's man, entered the old ballroom late that evening, Mrs. Formsby, the Lowestroft housekeeper, was already ensconced in one of the garden chairs as she sat before a roaring fire at one end of the room.

"I take it we are the first to arrive?"

Mrs. Formsby nodded and shifted her weight comfortably. "The others are even now on the way. Mr Tilbin has volunteered his assistance to Nurse Rae should she need it." Further explanation along that line was unnecessary since to their ears almost immediately came the sound of slowed footsteps and the thud of the nurse's wooden crutches striking the old stone floor.

While Tilbin, the butler, and Carlyle, the earl's personal servant, were of high stature within the ranks of the castle servants, neither could be faulted for his sensibilities in helping to assist the injured nurse to a chair and to help in placing a stool so that her broken leg might rest in comfort. Mrs. Formsby, not to be outdone in sensibility, had brought with her a cushion and a patched but quite serviceable kerseymere shawl to drape over the nurse's legs, both for warmth and modesty.

Nurse Rae had just been comfortably situated when Perkins entered, bringing with him Weems, one of the undergardeners. That person appeared nervous in the extreme. Not the least of reasons was that he found himself suddenly in the presence of the four most powerful and high-ranking servants in Lowestroft.

When Perkins ordered him to a chair, he sat on the edge as if ready for flight and nervously fingered his woollen cap. Carlyle and Nurse Rae appeared to be somewhat in consternation that a mere undergardener would be allowed to join their ranks. And even Mrs. Formsby appeared a trifle disconcerted. It was Tilbin, however, who questioned Perkins.

"He's got a story to tell and I think you'll want to be hearing it," Perkins announced. "Weems?"

"Well, I . . . uh . . . I didn't mean to be causing trouble and that's a fact!" Weems said nervously.

"No need for apologies," Perkins interrupted him. "Just tell the story the way it happened."

"Well…uh…well, it was like this, you see. I'd been separating some of the Iris bulbs—you know as how they multiply and if they ain't dug up and—"

"Get on with it," Perkins said. "Forget the flowers."

"Well, yes, but that's what I was doing there," Weems muttered. "And I've been hearing how there was this gentry-cove that wasn't to be trusted—"

"Yes, yes," Tilbin said, a trace of impatience in his voice. "Lord Battenton. Go on with the story."

This request from the august butler of Lowestroft seemed to give Weems renewed courage. "Well, it was as how I was working on the path and Miss Portney came by—mighty nice manners and all that," he said as if in not giving the young lady her due he might be insulting her. "I'd turned and gone back to my work, when along comes this Lord Battenton and there was a gleam in the man's eye..." He looked apologetically at both Mrs. Formsby and Nurse Rae. "Well, enough said. I...uh..." He paused a moment and then rushed on. "I managed to lose the grip on my rake, and it fell sort of across the path just as this cove was passing." Weems seemed unsure whether to be contrite or triumphant.

Perkins gave out with a bark of laughter. "Tripped him up and he fell flat on his face on that muddy, new-raked ground."

Nurse Rae nodded grimly, and Mrs. Formsby settled back and relaxed more deeply in the wooden lawn chair; quite informal and human smiles crossed the faces of both Carlyle and Tilbin.

It was the butler again who spoke first. "And you have accorded him the honour of joining our ranks," he said to Perkins.

"After what that basket-scrambler said to him, I feel he deserves it," Perkins announced staunchly.

Weems gave a sigh of relief as around the circle the others nodded solemnly.

Carlyle, a most worthy gentleman, but one prone to order, shifted in his chair, rose and strolled to the fire where he held out his hands and chafed them in the warmth. "As one most recently accorded the privilege now being offered also to this worthy fellow, I should be the first to welcome him. But I think since we could be called away at any moment, we'd best get on with the subject at hand. And I do not think we will find Nurse Rae in disagreement since being here causes her discomfort."

"As I've said before, discomfort is nothing if I can help my little gentleman," the nurse said staunchly. "But I do not see how this is to come about. Why do our plans constantly fail?"

For a moment they sat and stared at each other, considering the disasters suffered by Miss Amethy Portney and Lord Northford in the past two days.

Carlyle spoke slowly, "The earl is a gentleman hitherto quite capable of handling his exploits with aplomb. I attribute the accidents to the fact that so much of his attention has been turned on the young lady he has not been cognizant of things around him."

Perkins slapped his knee. "I like your thinking. If you're right, the battle's half won."

"But half isn't good enough," Nurse Rae announced with decision. "And I am convinced we must come up with some better way of getting them together."

"What about the evenings?" Perkins asked. "The little fellows are in bed, and the drawing room is better for lovemaking—begging the ladies' pardon—than a farm cart."

Tilbin cast his eyes to the ceiling. "Obviously, Perkins, you do not spy at the windows. Lady Battenton makes the situation intolerable."

"Even my lord has taken to retiring early," Carlyle added, "though tonight all the gentlemen have deserted the ladies for the squire's card party."

"It's a shame we cannot manage some gathering of a pleasant nature," Nurse Rae persevered. "If the young lady continues to be trapped under roofs, dropped in ditches and any number of other unthinkable situations, she will develop a distaste for the earl."

Another round of solemn nods greeted her statement and as was her custom before speaking, Mrs. Formsby shifted her considerable bulk in the chair, thus giving warning of her intention to utter a statement of some import. "The problem as I see it," she said, "is their inexperience with children. We must bring them together while the children remain in some other adult's care."

The other five agreed, but they were some time in argument as to how to bring this about. It was Tilbin who came up with a solution.

"Lady Susan," he said. "I will remind her that tomorrow afternoon she planned to take the children into the garden."

"But it seems to me," Perkins objected, "that getting rid of the little fellows is only half the problem. Once it's done how do we get Miss Portney and his lordship together?"

"Oh, I don't think we need worry about that," Carlyle said, smiling secretly as he sat back in his chair and steepled his fingers. "We'll give them the freedom and opportunity and let things take their course naturally."

CHAPTER SIX

THOUGH AMETHY EXPECTED to be late to breakfast the next morning, when she entered the room only three people were present. Lady Susan sat at the end of the table in her accustomed place, partaking of a hearty meal. At her side, General Duckworth was interspersing the breaking of his fast by telling her one of his involved stories while Lady Susan seemed enwrapped in a calm solitude as if she were the only one in the room.

"Dashed impertinence of those American colonials," General Duckworth was saying. "Shooting from behind trees like the savages they have over there. Still—" he fingered his long, full sideburns as if surprised "—dashed fine shots . . ."

As he looked up towards Amethy, his eyes lighting as though he might have another listener for his tale, she gave him a smile and a wave and turned hurriedly towards the breakfast board. Lord Northford was idly looking over the fare provided for the house party's breakfast. He espied Amethy and waved her over.

"Come help me make a decision. I'm a ham person, but this sirloin looks singularly appetizing this morning."

Amethy pursed her lips as she looked over the fare that would have done credit to any London chef. She raised her eyes to the bright sunlight falling in the window and laid one pert finger against her cheek. "For myself, I think this is a kipper day," she said.

Northford's eyelids lowered to a sleepy nonchalance as he, too, appeared to survey the morning. "You might consider another factor," he said calmly. "The weather warns that imminent danger may lurk on the bright horizon."

"How so?" Amethy looked up, not at all sure what he could mean.

"I have personally given orders that should those brats escape the nursery again today, I will have every head in the household. But I doubt the ability of the entire British army to keep them where they should be. I've placed a footman on every door, a gardener at the foot of the oak tree and threatened both nursery maids with deportation in chains." He turned thoughtful. "But I've an uneasy feeling that I've overlooked something."

"Fie upon you, sir," Amethy said, laughing as she signalled the footman to serve her the kippers and a golden brown roll. "Are you saying a man of your experience and expertise cannot forestall three small children?"

Lord Northford, deciding on both ham and sirloin, gave her an arch look. "My dear Miss Portney, neither your record nor mine has been perfect as to date."

"I beg to disagree with you," Amethy said as she started for the table. "Our records have been unblemished, or more correctly, should I say perfectly blemished?"

Since they were engaged in conversation, the footman placed Amethy's plate on Lord Northford's right. They had taken their seats, when the smile he gave her took an impish twist.

"I suggest we forgo our banter and get this meal over as soon as possible," he said. "Apparently we will have at least two bites free of complaining sauce à la Lady B."

Amethy was in complete accord with Northford and felt his patience under the circumstances had been great indeed. They were no more than seated when the object of his displeasure and dread entered the breakfast room immediately followed by Lord Battenton and Miss Ruth Oglethorpe. Neither Lady nor Lord Battenton were at their best in the morning, a condition Amethy had noticed on previous days.

Lord Battenton, from pride in his social manners rather than friendliness, greeted everyone. His good-morrows were clipped and perfunctory. Lady Battenton deigned to nod and did not speak until she had approached the board and walked its most opulent length with an eye of disdain.

"Indeed, dear Ruth, I'm afraid you have little to choose from again this morning," she said, her voice high in irritation. "With your sensibility, I know you will be pleased to return home where your breakfast will be brought to you as you like it in your room. I don't presume to mention my feeling, for child, if you can suffer without complaint, I'm sure I must not regard my own sensibility and discomfort."

Northford, both irritation and humour showing in his eyes, leaned slightly towards Amethy, his voice low. "Would you care for another fork, Miss Portney? Quite possibly we could eat with both hands and then leave the room most expediently."

"I will not take your manners to task," Amethy replied with a twinkle in her eye. "I do feel, however, that should a general exodus be made, the discomfort on Miss Oglethorpe's face would put her in the lead.''

Nor did the arrival of Lord Edgemere in the breakfast room relieve the young lady's depression. The young gentleman glowed upon espying the object of his *tendre*, but he received only the briefest of nods.

Amethy sighed, disheartened to think the lovers had been separated by some disagreement. Certainly, there had been little time for a problem to develop. On the evening before, the gentlemen of the household had ridden out immediately after tea to attend a card party given by a local gentleman. Only Lord Halstead had forgone the pleasure, spending the evening with his wife.

While Amethy was thinking of the young couple and their problems, her uncle entered the room, filled his plate and, at Northford's invitation, took the seat directly across from Amethy. His greeting was singularly dispirited, and after asking about Amethy's health and passing a few desultory words with Lord Northford, he turned his attention to his food.

"Buck up, man," Northford said, an indulgent smile on his face. "You look as though the roof on your favourite barn had just fallen in."

Lord Halstead shifted, his eyes moving down the table to where Lady Battenton's incessant complaints were continuing. "Dashed impertinence for Mary and I to put ourselves on you like this," he said shortly.

Lord Northford's gaze met Amethy's and then moved down the table. "I'd lay impertinence on other heads," Northford said shortly. "And I've been meaning to speak to you. I hope you'll earn your board and keep."

His suggestion surprised Amethy, but for some reason it brought a glitter of humour to Lord Halstead's eye. "Eh?" he said with more spark than he had heretofore shown. "To muck out the stables, am I?"

Northford grinned. "Something much more valuable. I'm starting a new drainage project. I'm wondering if some day you might have a look at it and give a word of advice—" Northford was not allowed to finish.

Lord Halstead was exquisitely sensible to what he considered the imposition of his family being at Lowestroft and was quick to jump at any opportunity to be of service to their host. "Glad to," he said. "I'm free this morning."

"Then it's settled," Northford replied briskly. "I'll have the horses brought around in half an hour." With that, he excused himself from the table and left the room.

Amethy warned herself not to let her feelings of gratitude to the Earl of Northford sway her wariness of the gentleman. But she could not but be grateful for the emotional ease he had given her uncle. She finished her morning's repast, rose and left the room and was approaching the stairs when a soft voice called her name.

She turned to see Miss Ruth Oglethorpe approaching. The young woman looked a bit harried as she glanced over her shoulder to make sure she wasn't overheard.

"The weather promises to be pleasant today," she said. "I planned to take my sewing into the garden. If you would like to join me, I would be pleased to have your company."

"I would be delighted," Amethy said brightly. "For I much doubt my aunt will want my company, though I must look in on her." With a smile she continued her way up the stairs, and Miss Oglethorpe turned into the gallery.

As Amethy had expected, her aunt, still recuperating from the travails of the happy event, was totally caught up in the wonder of the Honourable Cedric Tooms. She was being politely patient with anyone who interrupted.

After five minutes Amethy went to the nursery. The boys were engaged in a game of farms with their paper animals and would spend the afternoon playing in the garden under the eye of Lady Susan. Feeling unneeded, Amethy left the nursery. In the passage she came to an abrupt halt as she viewed a disaster much out of the commonplace.

The Lowestroft nursery maid, Maggie, was standing head down, receiving an angry set-down from Lord Battenton who bore upon his person the evidence of a spilled nursery tray. Milk dripped from his superfine coat. He was busily engaged in trying to wipe away globs of bread pudding that clung to his waistcoat and trousers. While his anger appeared to be justified, Amethy was caught by a certain satisfied expression upon the nursery maid's face, though her head was hung in submission.

Not wishing to intrude, Amethy hurried to the stairs and quickly descended. She could not help but wonder at the gentleman's presence on the nursery floor and decided he must have been exploring the castle.

Amethy knew Miss Oglethorpe was in some emotional agitation, so after procuring a shawl and her sewing basket from her room, she hurried to the garden where she found Ruth sitting in the same sheltered area as on the day before.

"Such a pleasant day," Amethy said as she seated herself and dug from her basket the package of needles she had discovered in her hatbox. "I declare I am jealous of every moment I do not spend in the sunshine."

Ruth nodded a halfhearted agreement and kept her eyes turned to her sewing. Clearly her mind was on other things, and she was making several tries before she set each delicate stitch. Twice she took a deep breath as if preparing herself to speak, but each time her courage seemed to fail.

After the third such incident, Amethy brought up the painful subject.

"It cannot be thought less than wonderful how the heart can raise one to the heights one moment, then cause such distress another."

Ruth Oglethorpe looked up, fear in her dark shy eyes. "Is it there for the world to see?" she asked.

Amethy thought it most certainly should have been, but she shook her head vehemently. "But do remember, being in your confidence, I would be more aware than most."

This assurance relieved the young lady, but now that the subject was out in the open and she could give the front of her mind to it, the pain in her eyes deepened.

"Robert is in no wise at fault," she said quietly.

Amethy viewed her for some moments in silence. Then her thought tripped off her tongue before she could stop it. "You do not impress me as one who would toy with another's affections," Amethy said.

As is often the case, a show of sympathy brought the tears to Ruth Oglethorpe's eyes. The handkerchief, not yet hemmed, was put to use to wipe away the two sparkling drops that rolled down her cheeks. "The cause is just," she said. "My uncle is a man of suspicious nature."

"And if you married, he would not be able to use your fortune..." Amethy hesitated, feeling she had said too much. One did not criticize another's relatives with impunity.

Miss Oglethorpe carefully set several stitches. "It is disloyal of me to speak ill of a relative—" she paused gathering her courage "—nevertheless, your assessment is correct. And should I marry, my uncle will most certainly lose that which he most desires. He is not one to give up easily."

"Gammon," Amethy snorted in a manner most unladylike but one that did sufficiently express her sentiments. "What can he do? I much doubt you owe him anything, and no one can force from you what is yours unless you allow it."

Ruth's needle had been busy setting stitches that she would later be most reluctant to allow anyone to see; she looked up with tortured eyes. "I think that would be true of you, Miss Portney," she said slowly. "You do appear to be a person of infinite resource and strong character. Alas, I know myself well enough to be sure I'm not. While I find claims of excessive sensibility most odious..." She paused in confusion, but there was in her expression the feeling that once she had said something quite disloyal to Lady Battenton it was done. She took another breath.

"I cannot cope with unpleasantness. I become physically ill."

"Then you are in the wrong household and should leave it as quickly as may be," Amethy announced with decision. "And in only a few days, you may do so."

At this, Miss Oglethorpe dropped her sewing and wrung her hands in futility. "It is my fondest dream, but I have no relatives with whom to take shelter. I could not even depend upon the company of my maid. I believe she is set upon me as a spy so my uncle might put a stop to any connexion I might make."

"But you need not leave," Amethy objected. "You could remain at Lowestroft with Lady Susan. Or when we return to Halstead, you would find a most genuine welcome there."

Even as Amethy was speaking, Ruth was shaking her head.

"I could not. Lady Battenton is in dread of my uncle's creditors latching upon her fortune. She is anxious for his plans to go forward for her own protection and is closely connected with Lady Susan and several important families in the neighbourhood. Anyone in this part of the country who sheltered me against her wishes would be decidedly uncomfortable."

"I seriously doubt that Lord Northford or Lady Susan would care a fig, and you need not remain long," Amethy said, continuing to press her point. "A note to your man of business should be sufficient not only to procure the funds for travel, but he could find for you some elderly woman who would act as chaperone in return for a decent allowance and a nice home."

"I've thought of it—I wish I could do it," Ruth said. "But no one must suffer at my expense. I cannot see a solution to my problem."

"Have you discussed it with Lord Edgemere?"
Amethy asked. "Mayhap he has a suggestion."

The pain returned to the young woman's eyes. "I
dare not go near him. My uncle has threatened that if
I am seen in Robert's company again, he will remove
us from Lowestroft." Her face turned wistful. "Miss
Portney...?"

"And that is why you were so cold to Lord Edgemere at breakfast?" Amethy asked.

Ruth nodded numbly. "And I could not even give
him a hint as to why my feelings have apparently
changed." That wistful look came back to her face
again as she stared at Amethy.

Suddenly the reason for the invitation to join her in
the garden became clear. "And you wish me to carry
your sentiments to him," Amethy said quite abruptly.

Ruth dropped her gaze back to the unfinished
handkerchief in her lap but said nothing.

"It's no imposition, I assure you," Amethy's sympathy caused her to add. "If I can aid you, I will be
glad to do so."

She would have said more but the young lady's eyes
were so full of gratitude that Amethy found herself
overbrimming with humility.

Amethy would have been willing that very moment
to go in search of Lord Edgemere. But she knew he
had ridden out with Lady Susan and General Duckworth again and was not expected to return until luncheon.

They sewed companionably until a footman came
to apprise them that luncheon was soon being served.
Both young women entered the dining room, hopes
high, that Amethy's opportunity would come quite
soon.

To Amethy, the meal was totally without interest for as Tilbin explained to Lady Susan, Lord Northford would be away until midafternoon.

The rest of the house party was gathered, the conversation wholly controlled by Lady Battenton, who had made a happy discovery of a local modiste capable of creating the newest London fashions.

The luncheon party heard of the placement of every pin until they were heartily tired of the subject. But Amethy was glad they were relieved of Lady Battenton's constant complaints.

As luck would have it, Lord Edgemere happened to be the first to leave the dining room, and Amethy, desirous of catching up with him as soon as possible, hunted back and forth throughout the main rooms of the castle.

Added to her frustration was a message brought by one of the footman requesting her attendance on her aunt when it was convenient. She hurried to the guest wing and found her aunt once again in slumber. Her frustration grew when she returned to the ground floor of the castle and was then caught by Lady Battenton. The woman was not completely wound down on the subject of the new modiste and kept Amethy in conversation for quite fifteen minutes.

By that time more than forty-five minutes had passed since the luncheon party had broken up and Amethy was in a fever of frustration. Risking gossip, she approached Tilbin with her problem, making a lame excuse for wishing to see Lord Edgemere and asked him if he was aware of that gentleman's whereabouts.

Tilbin's answer seemed overly considered. "I believe Lord Edgemere is taking a walk through the bluebell gardens and into the wood, though I must say this is the wrong season for bluebells. However, there are certain fall flowers and a lovely lake.''

Amethy thanked the butler and hurried on her way. If she could find Lord Edgemere, her service to Ruth would be speedily completed and she could ease the young lady's mind. In addition, she would enjoy a walk. In the garden, she came upon a sight that caused her to smile.

Lady Susan and General Duckworth were seated in two of the garden chairs enjoying a companionable nap. Her ladyship's face was in the same repose as it usually held when waking. General Duckworth, too, bore a similarity to his customary expressions. Though soundly asleep, his mouth was open as though he were taking a breath to start another lengthy tale. His right hand rested on the arm of the chair with one finger outstretched as though he had fallen asleep in the midst of making a point.

Amethy paused, looked up at the castle, and shook her head. Lady Susan was to have brought the children into the garden for the afternoon, but apparently the lady's absentmindedness resulted in her forgetting all about the youngsters.

They should be enjoying the sunshine, Amethy thought, but when comparing their plight to that of Ruth's and Lord Edgemere's, she decided her duty lay with the young lovers and hurried on past.

She had left the garden and strolled some half a mile from the castle on a narrow dirt track when she came out of a small copse and saw a beautiful expanse of blue lake just to her right. Then surprise and fear rooted her to the spot.

Floating out on the lake was a small raft. On it, being slowly moved by the current, were three frightened little boys; Willy, Edward and Jackie.

They were calling out in anguish and dismay as the raft moved slowly along. Lifting her skirts, Amethy ran down the path towards the lake. The children espied her and their cries heightened.

She looked wildly about as she approached the lake and her cursory search was rewarded. She turned immediately toward what appeared to be a punt, dragged just far enough up onto the bank to anchor it.

She momentarily considered going for help, but the raft was caught in a current. The castle was more than half a mile distant, and by the time help arrived the children could be carried onto a river and be in serious danger.

Amethy was no stranger to the water and had no fear of taking out the punt. She was knowledgeable enough to know that the presence of a pole and the absence of oars indicated the lake was shallow, an ornamental sheet.

She had stepped into the punt and picked up the pole when the sound of hoofbeats nearby brought her eyes to the edge of the wood.

Riding down the path, and coming immediately to a stop, was Lord Northford. He took in the situation almost immediately and urged his horse into a gallop.

"Hold!" he called to her. "Wait for me."

He leaped from the saddle and dashed to join her in the boat, but his steps as he entered were far more cautious than hers.

"Take care!" he warned. "This boat is old."

"It . . . it was here," Amethy said in an attempt to explain, but his imperious gesture as he motioned her to one of the centre seats gave no heed to her problem.

His expert maneuvering of the craft took them out onto the lake. Amethy felt secure with his handling of the boat, but she misread the lines of tension around his face. Believing he was angry and thinking she knew the reason, she defended herself.

"You're going to say I should have gone back for assistance," she said. "But I was not aware of their danger until I reached the lake."

Northford nodded shortly, giving most of his attention and energy to poling the boat. "They were supposed to be with Lady Susan," he said. "At breakfast I told you I had overlooked something. I should have called out the army."

Several minutes later the punt bumped the side of the raft, and Amethy nearly unseated herself as she clung desperately to the rough wood, holding the two crafts together.

The children crawled to the edge and waited for Northford to lift them into the boat. All three were chattering at once until a manful order from the earl brought silence.

"Still and quiet," he demanded, his tone brooking no objection as he poled towards the shore. "When I want to hear from you three thatch-gallows, I'll tell you. Why did you leave the garden?"

Willy and Edward, unaccustomed to being spoken to in such short tones by such an august gentleman as the Earl of Northford, ducked their heads and remained quiet.

Jackie was chastised, but Amethy noted he showed no real fear of his guardian. "I wanted to see the baby ducks. We all wanted to see the baby ducks," he added, generously sharing the blame with his friends.

Edward, being the oldest, appeared to feel it behooved him to lay part of the blame elsewhere. "And the dock wath broke and floated away." His lisp was accusing. "On our lake, the dock thtayth where it'th thuppothed to be."

"There is a dock at Halstead Manor," Amethy explained to Lord Northford. "I can see how they mistook a grounded raft for a permanent structure."

Northford nodded. "But that's not the point—" he turned a fulminating eye on the three children "—you were to play in the garden."

During this time he had poled them about halfway to the shore, and the tension of the situation was now beginning to manifest itself in the earl as irritation. "I've half a mind to give all three of your bottoms a good warming and shut you in the pantry."

At his remark, both Jackie and Edward lowered their heads. But Willy, brave at the beginning of any adventure and fearful in retrospect, gave out with a wail. He stood up, trying to reach Amethy and stumbled against the side of the punt. Northford moved forward to catch him, forgetting his own admonition to place his feet upon the ribs. His booted foot came down hard on one of the old boards. The sound of splitting wood was immediately followed by Lord Northford's decrease in height by fully a leg's length, followed by the gurgle and rush of water into the boat.

Amethy and Lord Northford mirrored each other's expressions as their jaws dropped, knowledge of another disaster clear in their eyes. Neither moved as the wooden side of the punt disappeared beneath the shallow lake surface.

As the punt slowly sank to the bottom of the lake, Amethy stood and, because Edward was the closest, caught him up in her arms, keeping his head level with hers. Northford was holding both Jackie and Willy.

Amethy was unafraid. Instead, she was filled with a sense of utter futility.

Another disaster.

The children were too shocked to speak and were as quiet as the adults.

The water was more than waist deep on Amethy, but they seemed to be on reasonably firm ground. Lacking panic, both she and the earl just stood and stared at each other for moments before readying themselves for the trek to the shore.

Jackie broke the deflated silence. He looked up at his big cousin. "Nurse Rae is going to be mad at you," he said.

Amethy couldn't prevent her laugh. "I do feel the nurse will have some supporters," she said to Northford. Since she knew they were not in any danger, Amethy's mind turned to more practical matters.

"Sir, is your foot caught?" she asked, remembering that sickening sound of the splitting board that had caused their present situation.

Northford moved experimentally. "Apparently not," he said. "I'll take these two blackguards to the shore and come back for Edward."

But Amethy found the waiting quite as odious as the possibility of tripping, so she followed him. On the shore, all five tried to shake and press the water from their clothing. She couldn't believe it. How could this man get her in such predicaments? She imagined what Lady Battenton would say, and the injustice of the situation made her angry.

"Another outfit ruined, sir!" she told him. "I daresay it is well for your fortune that you remain in the single state. I am convinced, after having been a most unwilling participant in some of your escapades, that it would take all the modistes in London to maintain a suitable wardrobe for Lady Northford."

Northford glowered down at her as he tried to press the water out of his coat. His anger was increased as the doeskin breeches, like many leathers when wet, began to sag. "And you, madam," he retorted, "had best seek a husband of considerable fortune! For Weston, Harrington, Formouth, Shultz and Scott would be kept busy just supplying him!"

"Are you saying that this is my fault?" Amethy shouted. As she picked up her reticule and rose to her feet she ordered the children up the path towards Lowestroft and followed, her head held high.

Northford brought up the rear, and she had no need to see his face to know his mood. The tone of his voice sufficed.

"Madam, I lay not one iota of blame upon your shoulders. I will only say that until I had the misfortune to come into your company, the accidents, such as we have just suffered, were not a part of my usual experience."

"Then I will remind you, sir," Amethy snapped, "that I did not knock the supporting post out from under the roof, run the cart into the ditch, nor did I step through a rotten board in the bottom of the boat!"

"But you were there," Northford snarled.

"Only as a witness to your follies, my lord." Following the children, Amethy increased her pace. They were running up the path, anxious to seek the safety and security of the nursery after this last escapade. Amethy couldn't resist throwing one remark over her shoulder.

"And I should think a gentleman would be gallant enough to admit his faults without recourse to maligning others."

"Still looking for the knight in armour?" Northford called after her. "You should have had him with you today! He would have rusted solid before he reached shore!"

Disdaining to answer, Amethy increased her pace and caught up with the children. Jackie fell back to walk with her, his cold little hand clasping hers.

"Miss Amethy, can we have chocolate and sugar cookies when we get back?" he asked, shivering.

"We'll see what we can do," Amethy said, turning her attention to the children and ignoring Lord Northford.

What she could not ignore was the dread of the shocked expressions on the faces of the house party and the servants as the five of them returned to Lowestroft after another disaster.

CHAPTER SEVEN

THE NIGHT WAS HEAVILY OVERCAST, neither moon nor stars gleamed upon the garden outside the old ballroom windows. At one end, flames leapt merrily in the fireplace and cast shadows of the lawn chairs still gathered around its warmth. When Perkins and Holmes entered the room, they found Nurse Rae already there.

"Evening, ma'am. Tilbin help you in?"

The nurse looked complacent. "I'm managing quite well on my own, thank you," she said. "Any day now I'll be able to take over the care of my little gentleman again."

"Ha!" Perkins exclaimed. "You can use one of those crutches for poling."

At the nurse's questioning look, the head groom gave her the gist of the disaster by the lake.

While he had been speaking, Tilbin, Carlyle, Mrs. Formsby, Weems and Maggie entered the room. They listened while Perkins finished the tale and shook their heads mournfully.

Nurse Rae's lips drew into a thin line. "It's plain to see I must take my little gentleman back," she announced. "I'll not have him put into such dangers." She glowered at Maggie who had entered with Mrs. Formsby.

"I brought her," Mrs. Formsby said quietly. "Maggie has earned her right to come."

"Our numbers are growing," Tilbin said, looking about the room. "I, for one, am interested in why Maggie and Holmes are here."

Perkins, standing by the fire, squared his shoulders as if ready to do battle. "I'll be taking the responsibility for Holmes," he said. "He's got a tale that ought to be heard."

Tilbin cleared his throat a bit pompously. "We would, of course, be interested if it pertains to the subject of our gathering," he said, "but do keep in mind that we are here for a purpose."

"Oh, forgive me! I thought I could bring Holmes in to talk about the shoeing of a horse!" Perkins said, bristling.

"Speaking for myself, I would be delighted to hear what Holmes has to say." Mrs. Formsby folded her hands across her ample stomach. "But I will speak about Maggie's presence at the meeting first. Keeping events in order will give us a clearer picture."

She then told the tale of how Maggie, having discovered Lord Battenton lurking in the upstairs hall outside the nursery rooms, correctly surmised his purpose and brought about a creditable accident, spilling upon his person the contents of a jug of milk and three dishes of bread pudding.

The rest of the gathering congratulated Maggie on her quick thinking, and while she blushed they assured her that the set-down she had received was in truth a badge of honour.

"Ah, 'twas nothing," the blushing Maggie replied.

Carlyle, that most august gentleman's gentleman, cleared his throat in preparation to speaking. "I see danger in what we are doing. As we thwart Lord Battenton's attempts to catch Miss Amethy alone, the situation grows steadily more ominous." He steepled his fingers and moved his head so the pince-nez reflected the firelight. "From what I have heard, this gentleman is most assiduous once he determines his course. We must keep a very careful eye on Miss Amethyst Portney."

The others nodded solemnly, then Perkins cleared his throat, developing a technique to match that of the top-lofty gentleman's gentleman.

"The best protection for the young lady," he said, "would be to get herself and his lordship together. I take it the plans of Tilbin and Carlyle were put into effect, since both his lordship and the young lady went into the lake together."

The nods in the group showed resignation.

"Well, one good thing did come of it," Perkins said. "I think it's time for Holmes to tell his tale."

Holmes's cheeks turned red, and he shuffled a bit before he started his story.

"It was a bedraggled bunch that came up from the lake," he said, shaking his head. "And that little gentry-mort was mad as a wet hen. And his earlship came into the stables, shouting we should bring out some clean horse blankets."

"Oh, my poor little gentleman," Nurse Rae wailed. "And me not there to properly dose him to keep away an inflammation of the lungs."

"I took care of that," Maggie spoke up. "Doing it just as you did not a month ago," she said.

Nurse Rae, her fears somewhat assuaged, leaned back in her chair while Holmes went on with his tale.

"The little gentry-mort took the two Halstead boys and stormed off towards the castle. The earl, once he'd wiped away most of the water, picked up our little duke and started off and that's when I heard it, me not but a few steps away from the door."

"Heard what?" Carlyle prompted, too interested in the tale to remember his preliminary "Harrumph."

"Well, what I seen and heard was our little fellow giving his lordship pepper for fussing with Miss Portney. His Grace told Lord Northford she might take snuff and go away—them not being his words," Holmes added hastily when he saw Nurse Rae's shocked expression.

"Get on with it," Perkins urged him.

"His lordship told the boy that visitors did leave, and that's when our little scamp—his Grace—said he didn't want her to go. He said if the earl was to marry Miss Portney, he'd have a mother, which was what he wanted more than anything in the world."

The three women in the room gave out with simultaneous gasps.

Tilbin, the butler, leaned forward in his chair. "And?" he demanded.

"Well," Holmes said slowly. "It was the look on the earl's face I most remember. He faltered in his walking and looked at the lad as if he'd never had any idea the little tyke might feel that way. He walked on a bit—I couldn't hear what he answered."

"You couldn't hear?" Mrs. Formsby lost her normal complacency.

The male servants, even including Carlyle and Tilbin, gave snorts of disgust.

"It weren't for me to eavesdrop," Holmes said by way of explanation.

"No, it wasn't," Perkins agreed roundly, his face split in a smile. "But it seems to me the big task is done...." His eyes circled the room, moving from face-to-face. "The idea of marriage has been put in his lordship's mind—put there by the one person he can't send to perdition."

THE NEXT MORNING Amethy was just leaving the breakfast room when Lady Battenton peremptorily announced that Amethy and Ruth would join her in the gallery for a game of whist.

"Forgive me," Amethy said hastily, "but I fear other plans preempt my time. My hunter was brought over from Halstead Manor last evening and I must see my groom." Amethy felt she had been rude, but she was willing to appear so rather than to remain in Lady Battenton's company, and she hurried from the breakfast parlour.

Indeed, the chore she had put upon herself to escape the lady with her complaints was nearly as onerous as having stayed. Amethy was not a lover of horses. She admired their beauty from a distance. Their twitching noses, sudden starts, flexing of muscles and little nervous movements put Amethy as much on edge as the horses were prone to be. Her tenseness and that of the animal seemed to blend together and feed on each other until both she and the animal became nervous wrecks.

Nevertheless, she did feel it was her duty to visit the stable to assure herself Starlight was comfortably housed and at peace with the surroundings. This duty was far more an enforced responsibility laid upon herself than any true necessity. Stevens, the groom who had accompanied her animal from her father's properties, was responsible in the extreme.

And the trip must be made hurriedly, she thought as she left the castle and scanned the sky. The dark clouds rolling in on the wind promised a storm, and she wished to be safely back in the castle before any more damage occurred to her clothing.

A young stableboy directed her to Starlight's stall. "And, my lady," he offered, "if that big prancer would fancy some treats…" He brought her a bucket containing apples and carrots.

Amethy had fed the big mare one of the carrots when her eye was caught by a silhouette appearing at the door of the stables. Obviously Lord Battenton was about the same purpose. She gave him no notice and was engaged in giving Starlight an apple when a contretemps occurred and she turned to see what had happened. The words issuing from farther up the long building were enough to make her desire to put her hands over her ears. Lord Battenton was hopping about on one foot, cursing the little stableboy. On the ground between them lay a shoeing hammer, and the young man was mumbling his apologies.

Wanting to escape the foul language, Amethy looked about, espied a small doorway leading out into the stable yard and hurried through it.

Overhead the clouds were becoming ever more ominous. She hurried through the garden and towards the castle and had just reached the side entrance when the first drops of rain began to patter on the stone-paved walk.

Amethy was about to ascend the stairs when out of the gallery strolled Lord Edgemere. She was much struck by his woebegone look.

Looking about and making certain no servants were in hearing, she peremptorily accosted the young viscount. "Sir, I have need to speak with you," she said. "Could you join me in the small withdrawing room for a moment?" Ignoring the startled look in his eyes, she led the way across the hall, where under the stair a small unused room was vacant. The young gentleman did indeed resemble a squirrel as his hands twitched, and his chin receded farther into his face.

She led him into the room, held the door until he had entered and then closed it behind her. As she turned to face him, she found some difficulty in keeping her looks perfectly straight for the young gentleman stood stiffly, quite tense, as though expecting some sort of set-down.

"My lord," she said softly. "I am sent to tell you the disappointment you suffer is not at all real." The words were hardly out of her mouth when Amethy realized she had been in error for far from being reassured, the young gentleman stiffened and started to move towards the door.

"I fear, Miss Portney, this room is far too chilled and would suggest we return to the gallery," he said with a rapidity that would have tangled any ordinary tongue.

Not knowing what else to do, Amethy placed her back against the door. "Forgive me, I'm making a muddle of it," she said contritely. "I am charged with delivering to you a message and, sir, I am honour bound to do so." She hurriedly explained and though she thought she had handled it badly, her words had given him pause. He stood a moment staring at her, and then the hauteur upon his face crumpled into both misery and joy.

For a moment Amethy feared the young man would break down in tears. She left the door and rushed forward, placing her hands upon his arms. "Sir, do come and sit where we may converse without fear of being overheard," she urged. "I am convinced you would be better for hearing the whole story."

She led him across the room, and they took seats on the confidante close to the draped window.

"Forgive my boorish attitude," he apologized. "I am indeed glad Ruth—Miss Oglethorpe—has found a friend."

Amethy nodded. "Her uncle has developed some suspicion. She is in dread that he will take their party and immediately depart."

Lord Edgemere's hands clenched. "The rogue," he said. "Would we could simply give him the money, for my estates would more than support the quiet tastes of Ruth and myself."

"Admirable sentiments," Amethy answered. "But for myself, I am averse to rewarding the man's greed. I take it, sir, your desire is to marry Miss Oglethorpe?"

The viscount looked startled. "Did not Ruth say so to you?"

Amethy shook her head. "She spoke of a *tendre*. She did not advise me that the relationship was more serious than feelings of affection on both sides."

At that the gentleman seemed to take alarm. "It is my heart's desire to make Miss Oglethorpe my wife. To give her the protection of my name, my honour— my life. Would that her father had lived to know of my inheritance, then we'd have no difficulty today. But how to get around her uncle, I know not."

"Neither did Ruth." But she refused to end the conversation on a note of hopelessness. "There will be a way," she said briskly. "We must think about it. I personally can see nothing that will suffice as well as an elopement."

Lord Edgemere was quite shocked. "Out of the question." he said. "We would require a special license and I don't know where to procure one except in London, which is a two-day journey from Lowestroft. To take Miss Oglethorpe on such an adventure cannot but ruin her reputation."

Amethy looked at the young gentleman sadly. She was not a believer in flaunting the customs of society, but two young people stood on the brink of either disaster or lasting happiness and she found it quite irksome that both Miss Oglethorpe and Lord Edgemere tended to think only in the negative. Still, she had nothing more positive to offer.

"We will think of something." She rose from the confidante. "I will accept the charge to pass the message to Ruth that your affections have not changed." She left the room and continued towards her original destination, the nursery.

After the disasters of the past days, it was her intention to spend the day keeping the children absorbed in games, preventing an opportunity for any repeat of that week's disasters. She opened the door to the playroom, strode in and nearly tripped over Lord Northford who was sitting on the floor engaged with several pieces of rather odd-looking lumber. The breathlessness that came upon her could not be readily attributed to her climbing of the stairs or her brisk walk down the hall.

"I beg your pardon," she said. "I had not thought to find such a—" she looked at the odd pieces strewed about the floor with some confusion "—such a project in force," she ended lamely. Part of her discomfort came from the frown that creased his forehead as he looked up.

"I take it, Miss Portney, you and I are here on the same errand," he said.

Not sure by his tone of voice and his frown whether or not she was welcome in the nursery, Amethy chose to tread delicately. "It was my intention to keep the children occupied," she said.

"Then pull up that stool and lend a hand. This creation out of perdition in somewise fits together, and I'll be damned if I'll call the carpenter to show me what he had in mind! Hold this!"

Relieved to know the earl's ill temper came not from her presence but from the task he was attempting, Amethy did as she was told, pulled up the stool and held the two pieces he indicated at right angles. Together, as he had suggested she hold them, Amethy could see that the odd pieces of wood that had at first appeared to be rejects from the woodpile were indeed the sides of a miniature castle. A scattering of small carved and painted soldiers on the floor showed its reason for existence.

"Am I to take it, sir," she asked, "that the battle is over and the castle was destroyed?"

"None of your remarks, miss, if you please. The siege will begin when you and I have finished this project."

Amethy bit her lip to keep from smiling and held the pieces as she was so instructed.

Across the room, Edward, Willy and Jackie were busily parcelling out the soldiers. Seeing them engaged and not prone to climb out the window or sneak past her through the door, Amethy returned her attention to the efforts of the earl. While he was reaching about him, picking up certain pieces and discarding others, Amethy's gaze fell on a long rectangle, and its angle upon the floor made it immediately recognizable to the young lady.

She was seeing the bulky, graceless, but imposing tower of Lowestroft in miniature. Her gaze roamed over the other pieces, and suddenly the project made sense.

"I beg pardon, my lord," she said, "but I do see the difficulty. If you will but take—"

Lord Northford looked up with some asperity and interrupted her helpful suggestion. "My dear Miss Portney," he asserted. "I hardly think that a young woman who was totally put out of mind by a paper barn would understand this project." He reached forward, took from her the two pieces she had been instructed to keep upright and began trying to fit them together.

"Very well, if you don't need my help," Amethy said, removing her stool a little farther away. "I will just see if these pieces make any sense to me."

Amethy could not be faulted for the justifiable pride she felt in maintaining her air of composure. She had suffered Lord Edgemere's stuffiness and was now being told she had not the intelligence to understand the task upon which the earl was engaged. Only the most censorious of attitudes would have found any fault with her desire to show him his error.

She sat for several moments, her eyes tightly closed, bringing back to memory the different angles at which she had seen Lowestroft castle. A strong spark of devilment caused her to plan carefully. Her intent was not to accomplish the completed task as much as to throw the earl into a confusion.

She did so by taking the tower rectangle, attaching a tall, short wall to either side. Rather than connect the main portion that would give it shape and form so the earl would recognize the configuration, she fastened together one of the wings and put it to the side. Next the square portion she had pointed out to him she stood upright, reached over and pulled from his unresisting fingers one of the walls and by means of the pegs jutting out from the corner bartizan, she slid the two together.

Her movements then were arrested by the look he gave her. "You devil," he breathed, speaking so softly his voice would not traverse the room and reach the ears of the children. "You see something I missed."

Amethy, her eyes overbrimming with laughter, strove to keep her face straight. "It is often the case, my lord, that those most familiar with something no longer see it."

Northford's eyes darted across the room, then back to the pieces of wood scattered on the floor. Understanding lit his face. He, too, fought to keep away a smile, but wells of humour deepened in his cheeks. "You won that one, Miss Portney. But I warn you, be prepared for another bout," he said, his voice low.

Amethy raised the tower that stood, when erect, over three feet high, attached another solid corner so that Lowestroft was immediately recognizable in the unfinished shape and sat back letting him complete the task. She chided him on the remark that had irritated her previously.

"There is a deal of difference, sir, between a paper barn and a castle," she said. "Now should it have been a stable and far less recognizable . . ." She faltered as all the humour left his face and he threw her a dark look.

"Is it the stable that interests you, miss? Or Lord Battenton?" he asked. His voice had turned cold.

Amethy was far too surprised to even consider a defence, and she stared at the earl in wonder. "L-Lord Battenton?" she stammered.

She had been shocked a moment before, but her anger was quick to follow. "My lord," she said coldly, "so there is no misunderstanding, I will explain this once and once only. Lord Battenton has never spoken to me outside a quite proper gathering, nor do I have any reason to assume he should wish to do so. I fear it is your own past that causes you to doubt him."

He looked as if he were about to speak, but Amethy hurried on forestalling him.

"I misdoubt there is any way we could be faulted for being in the stable at the same time."

"Then I most humbly beg your pardon, Miss Portney. Obviously I misunderstood the situation."

Amethy was in no way reassured that Northford believed and accepted her explanation, but she stubbornly refused to defend herself any further. Nor would she retreat from his disapproval.

She sat stiffly while, with an energy unwarranted by the project, Northford picked up the pieces and joined them together with a force that made her cringe for the small dowels.

Apparently he had expended his anger with his energy, for when the last piece of the structure was fastened together, he sat back on his heels and gave her a speculating look.

"That, I feel," he said, nodding to the finished product, which stood nearly four feet square and three feet high, "is sufficient proof that once I get the idea I carry the project to fruition."

Amethy nodded, more than glad to let the argument pass. "Ah," she said, "but what is a castle without people?"

"Just so," he said, looking up at her, his eyes suddenly intense and disconcerting. Then he seemed to catch himself up and turned to where the children were gathered in front of the fire, lining up the toy soldiers for a field battle.

"All right, brats," he said. "Let's populate this monstrosity.

Not loath to do so, the three children gathered up their soldiers and brought them to the miniature castle.

"It's Lowestroft!" Jackie shrieked as he looked at it.

"You defend the castle and we'll attack," Willy said.

For a few moments both Northford and Amethy sat quietly as the children deployed the toy soldiers. Then Northford, disapproving of Jackie's tactics, intervened.

"Here," he said, reaching over and moving two blue-coated figures. "You've left this wall undefended. Now if you put one guard here and one here—" he placed each of the soldiers on the corner watch stations "—at least you can protect your flank from a surprise attack." At the last words, he gave Amethy an ambiguous look.

Amethy was well versed in tactics. She had grown up playing endless games of chess with her father. She wasn't sure she understood the meaning of Northford's look, but she knew he was offering a challenge. She reached over, took a mounted soldier from Edward's formation and quickly placed him inside the hinged entrance gate that Northford had left open.

"Yes, do be careful of your flanks, your Grace," she said brightly. "And while you're watching them, you might give a thought to other vulnerabilities."

Northford's brows snapped down as he frowned at the enemy within the walls. Hurriedly he took two archers and placed them on the battlements above the gate, their bows pointed inward.

"One should not be too brave and daring," he warned her. "To venture boldly into unknown territory can lead to disaster."

Was he referring to the stable again, she wondered, to her attempt to find the children in the wood or did he have some other deeper meaning in mind? Whatever his intention, the challenge had been given, accepted, countered, and the next move was hers.

She took three archers from Edward and placed them in front of the castle at what she judged to be an adequate bow range. "But one should never turn one's back on one's enemy," she answered him. "And who knows whether or not the single foray is unsupported." With that, she aligned three riders in the gate, supported by her first entry.

Northford was quiet for a moment, then motioned to Jackie to hand him several of the small figures not already deployed. "I can see I face an enemy who will go to any lengths to win the day," he growled, and populated the walls with a strong defence.

Amethy, not willing to give up the slight advantage she had gained, similarly occupied herself by placing archers around the most heavily defended areas.

"How about here?" Edward asked.

"No," Amethy replied shortly. "Never waste efforts on the impossible."

While she was thus engaged, Northford had moved around to the rear of the miniature castle and stepped into the small opening, where the human defender could most easily deploy his defence. That occasioned the necessity for Jackie to remove himself, and Northford, in a surprise move, leaned forward and shut the gates between Amethy's lone intruder and the support from without.

"One should solidify one's position," he said smugly.

Amethy, not expecting such a dastardly deed, sat back on her heels. Then, in a decisive move, she brought in archers for defence and lined several soldiers up in the position they would normally take if handling a battering ram.

"If one should take action not one's right, then one must expect strong opposition," she announced.

Northford moved up heavier reinforcements for the front wall of the castle. "Force can only be met by force." What was meant by his sudden change of voice, from the triumphant to soft charm, she wondered. Then decided she must have misheard it. They were engaged in a war after all.

Since neither Amethy nor Northford were willing to give an inch, the deployment of the soldiers took all of their attention. Amethy had ceased to worry if there were hidden meanings behind Northford's words; once fairly joined in battle, she was determined to win though he had the advantage of the protection of strong walls.

She had not noticed when Edward and Willy ceased to hand her the soldiers needed for an active assault. She reached out to gather in the last of her warriors, when she stopped suddenly, looking around. She and Northford were the only occupants of the room.

When he realized her attention was elsewhere, he also glanced about and sat back on his heels. "Oh, Lord!"

Amethy jumped to her feet. "They didn't get out this door," she said.

Northford looked towards the window, rejected the tree as an avenue of the latest escape and stood, looking around. "I wager there's another entry to the hall from an adjoining room."

With Amethy treading almost upon his heels, he passed through the little duke's bedroom and on into another apartment obviously that of the nurse. They discovered the door into the passage standing ajar.

Trading looks of frustrated sympathy with the earl, Amethy shook her head. But this time he was not willing to admit defeat. "We'll find those brats if we have to tear down every stone in Lowestroft!" he said.

He turned and walked across the room, and his hand was nearly on the bellpull when some thought appeared to give him pause and he jerked back.

"No! We'll find them ourselves. Another smug look from a footman or a maid and I'll either be turning people out without a character or retreating to save face," he said. "You take one side of this hall. I'll take the other. Don't miss any rooms."

Some minutes later, at the end of the passage, they again stood gazing at each other contemplating the situation.

"Are you sure, my lord, that we should not rout out the servants for a search?" Amethy asked.

"No!" Northford snarled. "What would interest those rapscallions—not the guest rooms. They'll either be in the public rooms, the tower or outside. You check below. I'll check the tower and the garden."

"But it's raining," Amethy objected. "Certainly they would not—"

"Who knows what they might do," Northford said, turning away.

CHAPTER EIGHT

WHEN NORTHFORD DIVIDED the search area between himself and Amethy, he strode off intent on his purpose. She descended the stair, bypassing the second floor. Like Northford, she didn't believe the bedrooms and dressing rooms would interest the children. The first floor was also bare of their presence, but remembering the little duke's love of sugar biscuits, Amethy was not dismayed. She found her way to the cavernous kitchen of Lowestroft.

"Yes, his little Grace is always overly fond of sugar biscuits," cook agreed, and turned to query several of the workers in the kitchen.

The chief confectioner, hearing those magic words, "his Grace" and "sugar biscuits," called a halt to the conversation and brought from his worktable a sheet of that particular delicacy still warm from the oven.

"Would you care to take some with you?" he asked. "Mayhap the little gentlemen would return to the playroom appeased."

Amethy gratefully accepted some half-dozen treats wrapped in a napkin and continued her search. Having seen no evidence of the children in the halls through which she had passed, she took another turning and soon found herself in unfamiliar surroundings.

By the looks directed at her by the passing servants, she was aware she was invading their territory but considered her purpose too important to be swayed. In a squarish hall with passages leading off in three directions, she paused, considering which way to go when she felt a cool draft on her feet. Looking around, she saw a tapestry moving slowly.

She moved on towards the passage on her right when her gaze was caught by a suit of armour. There was something to be said for a family so ancient and active in history that their antiquities could even be used to decorate the servants' portion of the house, she thought. And she was quite sure why this one had been relegated to a part of the house not usually seen by visitors. The sword scabbard was empty and so was the outthrust hand that should have held a spear.

Impatient with herself for thinking of such matters when she should have been concentrating on where the children could have gone, Amethy continued and was more than ten paces down the hall when she came to an abrupt stop. Intruding on her mind with a clarity unusual for a memory came the three-way conversation held in the coach on the morning they arrived at Lowestroft.

"Oh, yes, you must find a magic sword. No one can fight a dragon without one," Amethy had said, intending her remark to deter any efforts to enter the lower regions of the castle.

She whirled around and went back to take a better look at the suit of armour. It was from a time when such items were heavily decorated with both Christian and pagan symbols. Its owner obviously wanted to ingratiate himself with whichever power he might confront. Since the runes and charms were resplendent on each piece of the armour and on the sword scabbard, Amethy had no doubt the sword and spear, if there had been such, were as well protected.

She was standing, considering the matter, when Sammy, a young footman, approached. Amethy stopped him.

"Can you tell me if there has been a sword and spear with this suit of armour?" she asked.

The young man stared at the armour, considered a moment and then looked slightly frightened. "I didn't take it," he said. "I spent all the morning above stairs."

"If you tell me the sword and spear were here yesterday," Amethy said, "I know who took them."

The boy, still looking exceeding uncomfortable, nodded miserably. "They were in place this morning," he said.

"Come with me," Amethy ordered, now sure where the children had gone.

She quickly strode to the old tapestry, pulled it back and saw that it covered quite an ordinary door. From the light of the hallway and the gleam coming from below, she could see stone steps descending. More-over, upon the steps, she saw a straight line of scars where something sharp had been dragged.

"Find us some lanterns," she demanded of Sammy.

"There are several below stairs, ma'am," he said.

With Sammy leading the way, Amethy hurriedly descended into the cellars and looked about. They were, as far as she could tell, most ordinary, though how far they extended, she had no idea. Wishing to make sure she was well-prepared for any search she might have to make, Amethy had Sammy find two well-filled lanterns and light them.

A cold feeling in the pit of her stomach warned her that while she might be on the trail of the children, she had not yet found them and might be some time doing so. Still, she reasoned, the year was 1812. Torture chambers had been out of vogue for more than a century, and no doubt any dangerous part of the cellar had long ago been closed off.

Inexplicable to Amethy was the well-marked trail around the stone floor. The children were apparently circling from chamber to underground chamber, stopping at various places along the outer wall. It was in the fourth such area, where root vegetables were stored, that she descried the reason for the search.

She understood her foreboding. A door stood ajar, and the trail of the children led through it.

Amethy felt a slight prickle of fear as, by the light of the lantern, she could see the downward slope of a natural cave.

Behind her, Sammy shuffled his feet uneasily. "They went down into the dungeons," he said.

"There are dungeons," Amethy's voice cracked. But then taking a deep breath and stiffening her courage, she stepped through the doorway. "Still there is not much to fear," she said. "We do have this scarred trail."

She led the way, still confident she would soon find the miscreants. Three small children would not venture far into that darkness, she thought, even though they most likely carried a lantern or candles. Before much time had passed they would be terrified of the darkness in front of them and closing in behind them. Thinking of their fear drove her forward with greater speed as she passed passage after passage leading off on either side.

So intent was she on following the scrape marks left by the sword on the floor of the cave, that only Sammy's warning brought her up short in time to notice a sudden dip in the ceiling.

"Thank you," she said, looking up at the wall jutting down. Without his warning she would have received a nasty crack on the head.

"I would not have believed they could come so far," Amethy said. "I am beginning to doubt that this is their trail."

Sammy, who had remained almost silent throughout the search and had given Amethy no reason to believe the young man had two thoughts in his head, came up with a quite plausible reason. "If you'll forgive my saying so, ma'am, being smaller, they haven't been slowed by the low ceilings as we have."

"That's quite true," Amethy said, much struck by the thought, and she grew increasingly worried.

Periodically she had been calling out and receiving no answer. But still not disheartened she continued on her way for another long distance before hope of following the scratched trail to the children finally dissolved into near despair. The spear had been discarded, and around the next turning she saw the sword as it lay in the middle of the passage.

Much cast down, she stood and stared at the weapon. Ahead the stone floor showed no mark. She thought for a moment and then squared her shoulders.

"Sammy, you must return and bring help."

"Begging your pardon, miss," Sammy said. "But Tilbin would have my hide if I left you alone down here."

By his look, Amethy wondered if Sammy's major fear wasn't being alone rather than leaving her to her fate, but Amethy had made her decision.

"Follow the marks on the floor, and they'll take you back to the entrance. Bring others to help with the search. And Sammy, make haste. The children will be in terror," she said. And so will I, she thought, as he turned and went slowly back up the passage.

Loath to go forward, yet with the plight of the children driving her, Amethy continued, careful to choose the largest passages until she came to an intersection where the openings were of equal size. For a moment she was thoroughly discouraged. Then she retraced her steps, picked up the weighty hilt of the sword and turned back on her predetermined direction. She moved forward with added confidence as she dragged the blade behind her, continuing the trail. At every intersection and turning she paused, called out the children's names and stood waiting quietly, not even allowing the dragging of the blade on the ground to interfere with what she hoped would be an answer.

She had continued for what she considered another half hour, when she looked down and stopped. In front of her were two scarrings of the sword. Behind her, three trails stretched into the darkness. She was walking in circles.

Not knowing what to do, Amethy stopped, leaned against the cool but dry wall of the passage and set the lantern on the ground. She allowed the sword to drop. What was she to do now? she thought.

Words whispered down the passages. The voice was so low Amethy wasn't sure it wasn't the echo of her hope.

"I saw a light, I know I did."

"Willy? Jackie? Edward?" Amethy called.

"Miss Amethy. Miss Amethy," Jackie called tearfully.

"Couthin Amethy," Edward lisped, and from a side passage she saw the glimmering of a sputtering lantern.

She soon found herself grasped around the legs by six dirty little arms while three equally dirty and tear-streaked faces turned up to her, seeking assurance.

Unmindful of her skirt, Amethy knelt and tried to stretch her arms around all three children.

Once in the security of her embrace, Willy, with the fastest recuperative spirit, demanded Amethy remedy the situation.

"Amethy, I want to go back to the playroom now," he said.

The other two voiced their agreement with Willy's plan, and his Grace, with a foreshadowing of the authority that would one day be his, voiced his principal complaint.

"Willy and Edward said there'd be a dragon to fight," he told Amethy. "But if there was one, I think it ran away when it saw us coming. And it wouldn't have been a very big dragon anyway. Some of the places we came through were awfully small—and I don't think that was a magic sword—"

"It wath too a magic thword," Edward disagreed hotly.

"I don't think so, either," Willy said. "If it was magic, how did it get so heavy?"

"Oh, but it must have been a weapon of great power," Amethy said, trying to stop the argument. "Because even when you left it, it led me to you, didn't it?"

The faces of the four-year-olds took on a wide-eyed wonder and they both nodded. It was most assuredly no disgrace to admit they were wrong when presented with such irrefutable proof.

Amethy looked up and down the tunnel and placed one finger against her cheek as though she were thinking.

"I wonder where I might find three little gentlemen who might like some sugar biscuits?" she asked the area at large.

The mention of food, particularly sugar biscuits, carried its own magic. Since her dress was already dirtied and a flounce torn, Amethy sat on the rough floor and pulled a folded napkin from her reticule.

The children would be better able to handle the walk back to the cellars after they had their repast, and she used the time for thinking.

Should they stay where they were and wait for rescue? She decided not to. They could follow the trail of the dragged sword. Then she saw flickering against the walls of the caverns; another light was coming in their direction. Someone was swinging a lantern as he walked.

"Hello," she called softly.

"Finally," Lord Northford's voice echoed back to her.

His attempt at irritation was so tinged with relief that it was to Amethy a parody. His steps quickened as he came around the bend and approached.

"Thank God, you found them."

The three children, spraying crumbs as they tried to eat and talk at the same time, tried to voice their complaint about an adventure gone wrong, but Northford silenced them with a resigned but authoritative word.

Looking up at him, Amethy's fears eased and she could not resist a laugh. "As I believe I've said before, my lord, our record is perfect!"

Northford, leaning against the outer wall some eight feet away, nodded solemnly. "I confess I cannot fathom this situation. I have yet to meet a children's nurse with more than ordinary understanding. It's not a vocation that requires wit. How do they keep these little beggars in line?"

"I have no idea," she said. "Either of us would starve if forced into that particular occupation."

"I beg you, don't speak of starving," Northford said. "I've missed my lunch and had no breakfast to speak of."

Amethy reached for her reticule and pulled out the napkin with the crumbled cookies. "Then by all means, my lord, let me offer you a repast."

Warily, as if some loathsome creature might crawl from the napkin, he took it in an outstretched hand and opened it.

"I fear the sugar biscuits got a bit crumbled in my journey, but that should not affect the flavour," Amethy said.

Northford tasted a crumb, nodded and then came to sit close by, offering to share them. "Should I ever again be lost in a cavern, you would be the ideal companion."

Amethy could not stop the warmth of pleasure invading her cheeks and, to keep it hidden, busied herself refolding the napkin and putting it back in her reticule. Northford, as if feeling he had said too much, rose and picked up both the sword and the lantern.

"Let's be on our way," he muttered. "Maybe we can get back before they send out a rescue party."

They had retraced their steps and were only a couple of turnings from the cellars when they saw a light coming in their direction.

Leading the party was Perkins. Behind him came Holmes, Lords Halstead and Edgemere, as well as several footmen and stableboys.

Edward and Willy saw their father in the train and dashed forward, grabbing him around the legs. They voiced their complaints of their cousin Amethy and the earl of Northford who had managed to get them lost again and had, in the process, not provided a single dragon.

Halstead, not to be fooled by his sons' efforts in their defence, focussed on them a baleful eye. "Up to your tricks again, eh, boys?"

Anxious as she was to leave the lower caverns and return to the comfort of her room, a bath and fresh clothes, Amethy's feet dragged as they approached the cellars. She dreaded passing through the castle. Her disreputable appearance would attest to one and all that she had been a part of another disaster, and even after reaching the seclusion of her room, she would have to face her maid, Carrie.

But it was not Carrie who engendered in her a fresh fear and a plan that brought with it a sense of loss. Nurse Kerns had overheard the tale of the children being lost in the caverns, totally lost her wits and had run to her mistress with the story.

Lady Halstead immediately called Amethy to her room, where the young lady was met with the suggestion that early the next morning, she and the children would return to Halstead Manor.

"I'm certain," Lady Halstead said as she sat up in bed supported by a number of pillows, "that nowhere on our property do we have the dangers encountered in this terrible place."

Amethy experienced a sinking of spirits. "I am persuaded I could no more handle the children at Halstead Manor than I can here. Think of it, Aunt Mary, today they escaped Lord Northford and I, both the Lowestroft and our own nursery maids. Butts and I alone would not be adequate for the task."

This seemed to give Lady Halstead pause, and before she could come up with another objection, Amethy hurriedly excused herself and left the sickroom.

On the way down to the gallery to join the house party before dinner, she determined to let no further problems occur. She must, she thought, remain at Lowestroft.

Ruth and Robert were in dire need of her help, and the thought of having to leave Jackie was painful. She brushed aside another impending sense of loss. Lord Northford, she told herself, was in no case a part of her reluctance to leave. Yet try as she might, she could not convince herself.

CHAPTER NINE

DINNER THAT NIGHT HELD all the exquisite discomfort of being lost in the caverns and none of the advantages. Her embarrassment was brought about by Lady Battenton's censure and was hers alone since the children were above stairs and Northford countered it with witticisms. Instead of recognizing his attempt to turn her from the subject she so tenaciously pursued, Lady Battenton's lack of understanding caused her to try even more forcefully to push her point home.

"And while I don't speak for myself, I do think there should be some consideration for Ruth's nerves. The poor child, living in hourly dread that some new disaster will befall members of the house party, is kept forever on edge."

"Doubtless from disappointment," Lord Northford said laconically as he accepted another slice of compote of duckling from the platter Tilbin offered. "To remain above stairs when such adventures are to be found below must be tame indeed, would you not say, Miss Portney?"

Amethy, brought into the conversation against her will, was caught between her desire to give Lady Battenton a severe set-down and to turn roundly on Lord Northford for baiting the woman. But she nodded decisively.

"Tame indeed," she said. "However, I will admit such adventures are not for everyone. For it can be uncomfortable indeed to bump one's head on the sudden lowering ceilings."

At the other end of the table, General Duckworth started one of his interminable stories, and finally the conversations moved to other subjects.

After dinner Amethy felt a need to be alone and strolled into the garden, but some moments later she was joined by Lord Edgemere. He wanted a sympathetic ear while he talked about his ladylove.

"Her life must be a complete hell," he said. "Would I could take her out of it."

"Then why not?" Amethy asked. "Tomorrow's sunrise will see her reach her majority. She is free to do as she wishes."

But Edgemere had already begun to shake his head. "I cannot blemish her reputation."

"I cannot see that you would do so." Amethy was impatient with the young man's negative attitude. "Have you no relative you could take her to until the marriage can be arranged?"

The viscount looked thoughtful, then again shook his head sadly. "None living close enough so we would not be on the road for days," he said.

"Have you friends nearby that you could reach within a day? Someone that would be sympathetic to your cause?"

The young gentleman seemed to think over the matter and his reply was again negative. He gave a deep sigh. "I cannot see how it is to be done."

"Miss Oglethorpe may be better situated with her uncle than she would be as Lady Edgemere." Amethy spoke with the force of her irritation. "What good does it do for you to speak of your love and yet quail at every suggestion meant to help bring about your happiness?''

If she had thought young Lord Edgemere to be spiritless, Amethy was soon to see her error. He rounded on her, his eyes hot. For a moment he appeared so resolute that Amethy could imagine him with a chin.

"Do you think I have not racked my brain in an attempt to find a proper solution?'' he demanded. "If I could provide her with proper chaperonage, we would be off to London tonight!''

"It occurs to me that I could provide both chaperonage and a maid.'' Amethy had spoken without thinking and not until Lord Edgemere turned to give her a look of such profound hope and gratitude did she realize she would be a slave to those words.

"Miss Portney,'' he breathed, reverence in his voice. "Yours must be the fairest heart in all existence.'' He dropped to his knees and grabbing her hand, placed a quick kiss upon it.

Amethy stared at the young viscount in dismay. She had been impatient with his stiff-front attitude, and this sudden turn towards the poetic, put her off entirely.

"Oh, do get up!'' Amethy said, startled and embarrassed. "Let us turn our minds instead to planning.''

Amethy and Lord Edgemere confined their stroll to a circular path around the flower bed, an area lit by the large windows from one of the castle's drawing rooms. They walked, supposedly thinking of the best way to accomplish the elopement. But in fact Amethy's mind was full of alarm and foreboding.

What would be the Halstead's reaction, and what would Lady Susan think of her? And Lord Northford's opinion? Would she be able to return to Lowestroft after taking part in such an escapade? Each hour at Lowestroft had become precious to her, not only because of Northford but also the wonderful little boy who needed her love. But knowing she could not leave the lovers in distress, Amethy resolutely pushed aside her own fears to plan the elopement.

"It would not do to leave in the night," she said decisively, "and risk an accident. If we stopped at an inn nearby, we could be easily overtaken in the morning."

Lord Edgemere nodded. "But how would we escape during the day? And what excuse would we give so no one would know we were leaving?"

Amethy's mind ranged forward over the plans she had heard made for the house party for the next few days to come. "Why, the hunt!" she said, her eyes widening with her own bright idea.

Suddenly the plans seemed to fall into place like children's blocks on the floor. Her uncle often complained that the only problem with the local hunt was the predictability of an old and wizened fox. The dogs invariably struck upon his trail, and he led them a merry chase but usually along the same basic path.

"Dashed sick and tired of Old Sandy," Lord Halstead was fond of saying.

But Amethy fervently hoped they would strike the scent of the old fox on the hunt.

Amethy outlined her plan to Lord Edgemere, whose eyes grew brighter with every explanation.

They had just stepped upon the terrace, planning on returning to the drawing room, when the garden door opened somewhat forcefully and Lord Battenton strode through. He halted, and the abruptness with which he ceased his approach led Amethy to believe he must have seen them from the window and had mistaken her for Miss Oglethorpe.

Before either Edgemere or Amethy could more than nod, Lord Battenton was followed by the Earl of Northford, whose leisurely pace and speech brought an easing of the atmosphere.

"There you are," he drawled at Edgemere. "Halstead's looking for you—you too, Battenton. He's demanding a rematch at the billiard table."

Edgemere, as overfilled with enthusiasm as he had been with worry, rubbed his hands together.

"He'll rue his challenge, won't he, sir?" In the élan of his new hope, he grabbed Lord Battenton by the arm and led him towards the door, but not before that gentleman cast a look at Northford that held such venom Amethy feared some harsh words had passed between them.

"Are you coming, Northford?" Battenton's question carried the weight of a command and increased Amethy's fear. Trouble between them could destroy the plans for the elopement, or could, if the Battentons suddenly left Lowestroft. But the tranquillity in Northford's voice put paid to Amethy's fear.

"Join you in a bit. I'll just have a word with Miss Portney and see her to the drawing room." He made it plain his remarks were private by taking Amethy's arm and strolling down the terrace, making no effort to speak until the other gentleman entered the castle and closed the garden door.

Amethy, embarrassed at the obvious ploy, turned towards the earl, determined to be done with a most deplorable situation.

Her practical nature suggested she follow in the wake of the departing gentlemen, but her heart refused. Knowing she was leaving Lowestroft gave a precious quality to those silent moments on the terrace. Northford was turning, leading her into the portion of the garden illuminated by the drawing room windows.

"I would have thought the adventure in the cave today would have given you a distaste of darkness," he said.

"Fie, when is a terrace in the evening to be feared?" Amethy said, laughing, afraid if she said too much she would give away her feelings.

Northford's gaze was unreadable, and after meeting his eyes, Amethy was forced to look away, lest he see in her own face the beating of her heart.

"You are indeed a remarkable young lady," he murmured. "At the risk of ruining yet another pair of shoes, will you take a turn with me in the garden?"

Like a dim echo, Amethy could hear Lady Battenton's censure if they were discovered, but knowing it might be the last time that she saw Northford alone, she closed her mind to any other opinion.

"And how not, since I am persuaded I will soon be totally out of footwear and forced to tread the halls of Lowestroft in my stocking feet."

"Should I have a pair of boots left, I would be honoured to place them at your service."

Torn between maidenly caution and the prompting of her heart, Amethy was both disappointed and glad when Northford eschewed the darker paths and circled the flower bed in the illuminated area. As if he read her thoughts, he smiled.

"We dare not risk a misstep. A torn hem or a spot of mud will be the end of us."

Amethy nodded. "We would not even be able to lay the blame on the children."

"No, and thank God they are not here!"

Struck by the vehemence of his tone, Amethy looked up, startled. Other than calling his ward "brat," Northford seemed to enjoy the children; certainly he never appeared to hold them in distaste. Could she be totally wrong about him? She felt pain that she had misunderstood him and thought perhaps it was just as well that she was leaving.

"I believe there was something you wished to say to me?" She felt she owed him the chance to speak, but once he had done so she would return to the drawing room or visit Miss Oglethorpe and explain the plans. She had forgotten in the past days the reputation of the man strolling beside her until his apparent antipathy for the children brought it back to her mind.

"Say to you?" He appeared puzzled by her question.

"I beg your pardon, but you did give Lord Battenton, Lord Edgemere and myself the impression..." She paused, seeing a smile soften his features.

"A bit of duplicity on my part," he admitted.

"My lord, I find you decidedly difficult to understand. Either you wished to have words with me or not."

"Not any precise ones," he muttered, irritation entering his voice.

Still unable to understand, Amethy could only assume he felt some need to chide her on her part in the disasters that had befallen them.

"If you had it in mind to speak to me about the incident in the caves today or about the children on the lake—"

"That was not my intention." His tone turned cold; he removed his hand from her arm.

As his defences rose, Amethy's became stronger. "Then, sir, will you express yourself so that I know just what I've done?"

"Of all the hen-witted—did it ever occur to you that a gentleman might care to spend a few minutes in your company without argument, without being surrounded by children or falling into a disaster?"

With that he turned his back on her, looking up at the castle. His profile in the illumination from the windows, showed an outthrust jaw.

Equally put off by the turn of the conversation, Amethy whirled around, intending to return to the castle by way of the other side of the flower bed. Unfortunately she had been facing the brightly lit windows, and her eyes were not adjusted to the dimness. She misjudged the width of the path.

"No..." she moaned as her right foot sank in the soft muddy earth.

"You didn't..." He approached her with rapid footsteps that came to a sudden halt.

"Oh, my God!"

His hand closed on Amethy's arm, but far from assisting her, he was in need of help to keep his own balance as his foot slid into the newly turned flower bed.

When they were back on the solid ground of the path again, Amethy looked up at the earl, tears of frustration bright in her eyes.

"One of us is cursed." She made a vain attempt to shake the clinging mud from her slipper.

"Just one?" Momentary defeat lowered his voice. His dejection was so like that of the children that Amethy forgot her own feelings and laid a comforting hand on his arm.

"Mayhap we can slip in and no one will know."

"My dear young lady, you are a trooper."

To her surprise he bent and kissed her softly on the forehead. Far from feeling his action was exceptionable, she saw his kiss as an addition to his somewhat unorthodox compliment.

With exaggerated care they entered the castle and succeeded in reaching the first floor without being seen.

As they reached the door to Amethy's apartments, Northford took her hand and raised it to his lips. His eyes were soft and warm as he held her gaze.

Amethy stood breathlessly, not willing to break the spell. She seemed to be swimming in her own happiness. As he turned away and moved down the corridor with exaggerated care, she opened the door to face an outraged Carrie, but for once the complaints of her maid drifted over her head.

Then she remembered she had been on the way to see Miss Oglethorpe, and after changing her shoes and stockings, she carried out Cupid's mission.

Ruth's hands trembled with excitement when Amethy made her privy to the plans. Her eyes were so bright Amethy felt they hardly needed candles.

"But your maid!" Ruth expostulated, looking doubtful. "It cannot be that she will agree?"

"No," Amethy said. "But she will come, and she never gives away my confidences."

LADY SUSAN HAD BEEN for more than thirty years an enigma to her friends and relatives. She appeared to have a most insipid nature, but she was in fact a woman of such an active mind that, while she heard everything said to her, her thoughts were too far ahead to be shared within the company usually surrounding her.

She was a watcher and reader of people and was too content within her own state to feel any need of explanation. The house party had, indeed, provided some diversion but had now begun to pall. She seldom heard all of General Duckworth's tales of his adventures in the Colonies, but she found his voice pleasant and his companionship agreeable.

It was a measure of her advancing age, she thought, that she could accept that gentleman with equanimity. Indeed she would be pleased to have his company indefinitely. They were sitting in the garden where he had begun one of his interminable tales and drifted off to sleep in the midst of it. But Lady Susan was restless.

Something was afoot.

A certain excitement had permeated the breakfast room. It somehow involved Lord Edgemere and Miss Oglethorpe, between whom her sharp appraisal had discovered a *tendre*. How that would bring Lord Battenton and Miss Portney into the picture, she had not as yet discovered. Both of them had been somewhat on edge, and their restlessness had communicated itself to her.

While the general sat sleeping peacefully in his chair, Lady Susan rose and strolled slowly about the garden, intending to give her attention to the need to refurbish some of the fountains. She was thus engaged and walking along a path by the outer hedge when she heard voices.

"And damned if I'll stand for it. Northford's put them to stopping me at every turn, and he'll pay for it."

Lady Susan recognized the voice as that of Lord Battenton.

"Well, I'll tell you, governor, I don't know as there's much as you can do about it since he runs the place."

"I can and I will!" Battenton replied. "He has his eye on that little piece, and she knows what's going on. She'll stand there prim as can be, telling everyone where she's going, and if being followed isn't what she has in mind, I don't know what is."

"That's as may be, governor," Lord Battenton's companion said hesitantly. "But there's never been any scandal attached to her name."

"Keep quiet and listen!" Battenton snapped. "You're to take the carriage, saying you're having one of the wheels replaced and meet me at the old ruin on Forharrow Road. I'll get her off from the rest of the hunt, bring her to the carriage and you're to take her on to Scarbourne Place. I'll see you along the way and then come back to the hunt."

"Lord luv you, governor, you can't kidnap a gentry-mort!" the servant gasped. "And even if you could, how do you know the hunt is going to go in that direction? I mean it ain't going to be easy trying to haul that gentry-mort cross-country if it don't go the way you think it will.''

"Don't concern yourself; I'll manage," Battenton snapped. "Northford's been putting spokes in my wheel since our salad days, and it's time I returned one."

Lord Battenton chuckled, and Lady Susan walked away.

She slowly paced along the garden paths and had it been her wont to be upset, she would have been enraged. Now that she knew of the plan, there was no actual danger to Miss Amethyst Portney if she told Northford of Battenton's plans. She could see some merit in telling Northford. He was attracted to the girl and she to him. Lady Susan had always been of the opinion that Northford should marry, and Miss Portney was a well-bred and amiable girl.

But allowing Northford to handle the situation would not give her the satisfaction she sought. With some imagination, Battenton could not only be thwarted, but Lowestroft would have its revenge on him.

Lady Susan was too much a Farringham of Lowestroft to meekly accept a slight on their house. To have a guest of the castle spirited away would be an insupportable insult and brought out a cold anger in her. The slight on the family and the house took precedence over a romantic affair.

Later that evening while dressing for dinner, Lady Susan surprised her maid.

"Can you, without raising suspicion, discover the colour and weight of the cloak that Miss Portney will take with her on the hunt tomorrow?"

"Uh...yes, miss," the loyal maid answered, her surprise in her eyes.

"Do ascertain if the young lady has a dark blue, lightweight cloak. If she does, do your utmost to influence the young lady to make it a part of her ensemble."

To this the maid had some rather strong objections. "Early afternoon will find rain coming down on the hunt, miss. At this season the young lady would be cold and uncomfortable, even likely to take a chill."

"Just so," Lady Susan said, nodding slowly. "And for just that reason, you will carry out my instructions."

"AND DASHED if I don't think we're going to fill the whole room before this is over!" Perkins said as he looked around at the assembled group.

To the original four, Tilbin, Mrs. Formsby, Nurse Rae and Perkins, five others had been added. The undergardener, Weems; the valet, Carlyle; the undergroom, Holmes; the nursery maid, Maggie; and now a stableboy, Stevens, who had joined the group by the singular honour of having dropped a hammer on Lord Battenton's foot.

"Hmm-hmm," Carlyle gave his usual clearing of throat and gathered to him the attention of the group. "I should think with such an august membership that we should now be able to bring our plans about successfully," he said.

Nurse Rae nodded. "For all the woman's flightiness, Nurse Kerns has left the lying-in room and is taking over the care of the children. I do not totally approve of that woman, but she will look after the little gentlemen."

"And I bring some good news," Tilbin ventured. "I was instructed just this evening to have two footmen ready to assist Lord Battenton's man in packing his trunks. The Battenton party will be leaving the day after the hunt."

"Fine! Fine!" Perkins cried. "Now maybe we can get on with this romancing. The way I see it, there can't be any more trouble now."

Nods circled the room.

CHAPTER TEN

ON THE MORNING of the hunt Amethy approached the dining room with both anticipation and fear. Knowing Lord Northford would be there, her pulse quickened; still she dreaded seeing him. If his mood of the previous evening had changed, she knew she would be thrown into a pit of despair.

Her worry was lessened when she neared the door. More than fifty people were milling about helping themselves to food from the enormous buffet. In such a crowd he would have no opportunity either to reinforce his affectionate remarks or to negate them. She turned her attention to the immediate problem of having breakfast.

The morning buffet was generous, but consisted of plain sustaining food that would carry the members of the hunt on a breakneck ride conceivably lasting throughout the day. Amethy stood for a moment watching the milling group. The Quorn and other famous hunts were limited to the upper regions of society, but like those of her home region, this particular gathering embraced nearly every available rider in the vicinity, regardless of his social station.

The squire, his wife and four husky young sons were at the moment in absorbed conversation with the local carter. The vicar was standing in the corner, listening to some verbal exposition delivered by the local innkeeper, who punctuated his remarks with a jabbing finger aimed directly at the vicar's nose.

Lord Halstead was at that moment engaged in an argument with a hireling from one of his leased farms. On the morrow, should the owner pass the property on which the hireling worked, the man would pull his forelock respectfully. But for the day, they were both members of the hunt, and their united purpose gave them a measure of equality.

Amethy edged her way through the crowd, nodding and smiling to farmers' daughters whose riding habits were clearly homemade. She smiled at shopkeepers from the village, who had closed their businesses for the day.

"Ah, another intrepid member of the party arrives," Northford said from behind her.

Amethy turned slowly, unable to prevent the happy glow that must show in her face. "Did you think, sir, that I would be so poor of spirit as to hide in my room on such an occasion?"

Northford feigned shock and insult. "Madam, could I be accused of believing you cowardly after having been witness to your search for dragons?"

"I pray you will not spread that story, sir," Amethy chided him. "Nor is it truly fair that you hold me in conversation, for quite clearly, we are in for an energetic day."

"By all means let us sustain ourselves," Northford said. His eyes lingered on Amethy's face and caused her colour to rise again.

Brought to some confusion, she moved farther down the table and once her plate was filled went to stand with Lady Susan and General Duckworth. Her mind was in a turmoil over the gentle remarks Northford had made the afternoon before, and obviously his mood towards her had not changed overnight.

But Amethy had little time to pursue her thoughts. Though she ate as fast as was seemly and possible for a young lady of her training, she was still not quite finished with her breakfast when the room emptied. The members of the hunt were filing out to mount their horses.

Amethy followed, wishing Lord Northford's description, "intrepid," had been more than a compliment. For Amethy, try as she might, had never been fond of hunting. She took no joy in the breakneck pursuit, though she was experienced in the sport. Her own father was an avid follower of the hounds, but he had raised Amethy to believe the gentry had a duty to take part in all local activities.

The day was overcast and confusion prevailed as the crowd moved through the garden, the hedge and out into an open field where the hunters were tethered. Every groom from Lowestroft and those from many of the surrounding properties were in attendance, but the confusion was so great that when Amethy located her mount, she found herself lifted into the saddle by one of the squire's half-grown sons.

Then came the inevitable chaos while the Master of the Hounds tried to control the pack, exhorting his whippers-in to bring order.

Amethy was unable to understand how word seemed to travel to every mongrel in the district that a hunt was taking place, but as usual, more than a score of uninvited dogs were ranging around the pack, barking in excitement, challenging each other and the leashed dogs, and creating a general confusion. The horses were restive and skittish, rearing and plunging in spite of the firm hands holding them back.

Interest quickened as one of the whippers-in drew an old wizened terrier from the pack and led her off on a leash longer than normal. The old dog ignored the raucous sounds made by the cursing and orders of the Master of the Hounds, the shouting and laughter of the riders. Less than half a field away, the old dog gave voice after locating the scent.

The mongrel dogs were first to give chase, followed closely by the loosed pack. The hunters, held on tight reins, bunched their muscles waiting for the office to start.

Starlight, Amethy's mount, normally a quiet animal, was nevertheless from a long line of blooded stock. She arched her neck, pranced and reared slightly showing her readiness for the adventure. Before Amethy brought her completely under control, they were off.

Most of the riders were shouting in exuberance, yet their voices were thin over the thunder of hooves. Despite her reluctance for the sport, Amethy could feel the pulsing of her blood as she shared the excitement of the start.

She was caught up in a mass of evenly moving horses and swaying bodies as the hunt followed the hounds. Gradually, as they raced across the pasture, the field spread out and they were fast approaching the first fence.

Amethy cast a worried glance to her left. Pacing Starlight was the ugliest, most awkward and raw-boned animal in existence. From the misshapen head to the knobbiness of the knees and the wide untrimmed hooves, the swaybacked creature appeared hardly fit to pull a plow.

On its back, wearing clean but much patched clothes, was a towheaded boy of no more than fourteen, some poor farmer's son, and his scrubbed face glowed with his love of the chase. She knew his days of feeding the stock, mucking out the stables and milking the cows were spent with the dream of the hunt in his heart.

The old animal could never make the upcoming jump, she thought, but knowing she could not stop the boy, all she could do was manoeuvre Starlight away from what must be a bad spill. No shout, no warning would reach through that bliss the youth was experiencing.

Amethy watched, her heart in her throat, as the lanky creature gathered itself for the jump. But the spirit that affected the young boy was also in his mount. For this one day, he was not an old plow horse, but a valiant steed worthy of any knight, lord or king. He cleared the fence with distance to spare.

And Amethy, so concerned for the boy that she had not readied herself, nearly took a spill. Only with tremendous effort did she remain in the saddle and Starlight, thrown off stride by her imbalance, faltered before continuing. So it was with some chagrin that moments later, she realized Northford was pacing her just to her right. His smile was sympathetic.

"You have to hand it to that old wolf bait. He can jump," Northford said. "I never thought he'd make it." With one hand raised in salute, he widened the distance between them as they approached a group of slower-moving riders.

"BUT IT GETS ALL in the way and knocks over my army," Jackie complained, watching sullenly as Nurse Kerns rearranged the pillow she'd put on the floor. He wanted Nurse Rae, not this Halstead woman. When he was busy playing, Nurse Rae left him alone.

But this woman kept pushing cushions at him, interrupting his war. She even made him put on a jacket. He was too warm if he buttoned the garment, and if he left it open the flopping coat tails knocked over his soldiers. His small jaw tightened, his lips pursed with irritation and he stood staring at the floor.

Nurse Kerns had considerable experience in caring for lesser young nobility, but the responsibility of the little duke terrified her. No fault must be found with her stewardship.

She had a good understanding of children, but nothing in her experience prepared her for the hundreds of years of implacable will born into the Lowestroft dukes. Theirs was a line that had caused more than one king to pale and finger his garments nervously.

In the slightly more than four years of his life, nothing had ever engendered in Jackie the cold anger and determination that now filled him and was as much a part of his inheritance as was Lowestroft or his titles. Born into him also was a strong dislike of being pampered and toad-eaten.

He missed his own nurse. Without her everything around him seemed strange, and the Halstead people didn't do things the way he liked them. Never having had any reason to deliberately thwart authority, Jackie was unaware there was such a thing as deliberate rebellion. Mayhap it was the wisdom of those ten generations of dukes that caused him to drop to his knees upon the cushion and offer no more objection to the interference of the Halstead nurse. No conscious thought warned him to await his opportunity.

It was not long in coming.

Both the nursery maids were off on errands when Agatha, Lady Halstead's personal maid, entered the nursery. She had a hurried discussion with Nurse Kerns, who said something about colic and came over to where the boys were having their war.

"Agatha will stay with you until Butts returns," she told the boys, and hurriedly left the room.

The lady's maid was in some agitation and paced back and forth between where the children were playing and the door leading to the passage. Finally, unable to stand the suspense, she turned to the children.

"Would you promise me to remain here and give the nursery maid Nurse Kern's instructions?" she asked of Edward.

Jackie, stroking the smooth flanks of a carved horse, was quicker with an answer.

"Oh, we promise to tell Butts as soon as we see her," he said, his active little mind taking giant steps on the path of duplicity. There was such a look of innocence upon his face that the lady's maid was at once assured her instructions would be followed and she hurriedly left the room.

Jackie remained quite still until the door closed and the sound of receding footsteps died away.

"Let's go to the stables," he said, jumping to his feet. "If anyone comes looking for us, Holmes will hide us. He never tells tales."

Young Willy was amenable to this plan, but Edward, older and therefore with a stronger sense of honour, put forward an objection.

"We told Agatha we'd tell Butth when she came," he said.

"As soon as we saw her," Jackie corrected, his giant steps on his new path becoming leaps and bounds. "And we will. We'll tell her as soon as we see her—when we come back from the stable."

Honour satisfied, they slipped along the passages and into the garden unseen, and were approaching the stables before they encountered their first serious obstacle. Two visiting servants were coming towards them.

Their only available shelter was a large hibiscus bush and they crowded behind it, kneeling on the damp earth in fear of discovery. But the approaching servants were too intent on their own discussion to notice the children. One of the men seemed to be worried.

"Argh, I'll tell you it means nothing but trouble—stealing a gentry-mort from the house party. And from what I hear about that Miss Portney, she'll be kicking and screaming all the way."

"And it may be as how I agree with you," the other man said. "But his lordship's given the orders. We've a choice to carry them out or be turned off without a character."

They continued to talk and much of their conversation was confusing to the children, but two points were perfectly clear. Someone wanted to take Miss Amethy away in a carriage. Jackie would not be able to see her again.

Something had to be done.

He sat plump on the ground and thought. The worst thing in the world would be to lose Miss Amethy.

"Ssh!" one of the men said. "It's Perkins!"

Jackie crept closer to the bush to hide from the groom while within his mind two thoughts warred. If he told Perkins what they'd heard, the groom could save Miss Amethy. But what if Perkins thought he was playing a pretend game and sent them back to the nursery?

While he was considering, through the hedge came Holmes. Perkins was just opposite the hibiscus bush when Holmes accosted him. The undergroom had also overheard the plot. He quickly told the groom.

"And I'm just for knocking those two thatch-gallows in the head and putting an end to it," Holmes said.

"No," Perkins said thoughtfully. "Let's put this to good use."

"Use be damned," Holmes said. "From what I've seen, Lord Northford fancies that gentry-mort. If he ever finds out we knew about this and let her come into danger—"

Perkins chuckled. "Oh, we'll tell him, but we'll let him save her," he said, breaking into Holmes's objection. "Best way I can think of to get them together. Saddle two of the fastest hunters."

"His lordship's own?" Holmes gasped. "He'll have us flayed!"

"Get 'em saddled," Perkins ordered. "If we head out now, he'll be on the trail in time to save her. She won't come to any danger. And what's better for getting them together?"

"It could be good for settling their problems," Holmes said. "But what happens if we don't find him?"

"Here's what we do...." Perkins and Holmes walked away so the children couldn't hear the rest of the groom's plan.

The three children sat on the ground and stared at each other. Jackie pulled a leaf from the bush and rubbed it as he considered the situation. Edward stared off into the distance, so Willy was the first to speak.

"I don't want them to take Cousin Amethy away," he said.

"I don't like their plan," Edward announced as he watched a small cloud. "Hen-witted."

"Perkins is not hen-witted!" Jackie threw down the leaf and objected hotly. Then he too became thoughtful. "But I don't like it, either. Suppose they don't find Northford? Or Northford doesn't find the carriage? Somebody's going to take Miss Amethy away, and I won't ever see her again."

At that Willy started to cry until his brother fetched him a halfhearted facer. "Don't be a baby! Babieth can't help."

That logic brought Willy up short. "I won't cry! I'm going to find that mean man, and I'm going to draw his cork."

"Yeah," Edward agreed.

"Yeah," Jackie confirmed, adding his approval.

How to accomplish this act of heroism immediately became the question in Edward's orderly mind and he voiced it.

But a brilliant idea had been born in the little duke's head. "They're going to put Miss Amethy in the carriage. Maybe we can hide in back; then when he brings Miss Amethy we can jump out and beat on him."

"I'm going to hit him and poke him and kick him," Willy said.

"I'm going to bite..." Edward, ever the logical, paused, put his tongue into the gap occasioned by the missing two front teeth and frowned. "I'll hit and poke," Edward amended the plan. "You bite."

The division of responsibility satisfactorily completed, they crept out from behind the hibiscus bush to reconnoitre that part of the stable in which the carriages were kept. There was no doubt which carriage was going to be taken out to abduct Miss Amethy Portney.

The vehicle stood alone in the yard, and the coachman had just completed sweeping it out and fluffing the squabs.

"Hurry," Jackie said to the others, and led the way to the back of the carriage. The luggage compartment was covered with a sturdy leather flap, attached to the roof at the back of the vehicle and extended down, fastened with straps and buckles.

While the other two danced about in a combination of anticipation and fear, Edward unfastened a strap at the side and gave Jackie an abrupt assist as he tried to climb in. Willy tumbled in on top of him, followed by Edward who reached outside and attempted to fasten the buckle again.

"I didn't get it quite hooked," he said as he quickly pulled his hands in because of the sound of approaching footsteps.

"Maybe no one will notice," whispered Jackie as the sound of the steps passed and faded.

"I wish we had remembered to bring the magic sword," Willy said.

Jackie nodded. "And I wish we had some sugar biscuits."

Very little light entered the luggage boot, and the small compartment was soon warmed by the bodies of the three children. Jackie watched his companions doubtfully as they drifted into sleep. He hoped they would wake up in time to help Miss Amethy. Maybe he would have to save her himself. While he was thinking of the possibility, his own eyelids fluttered and closed.

LADY SUSAN WAS an enthusiastic follower of the hounds and was usually one of the lead riders, but on this particular day, she had held back. More important issues were at hand.

She had been pacing Amethy Portney's slower and more cautious ride. Now she could delay no longer in putting her plan into action if she was to prevent the kidnapping of the young lady. She came abreast of Amethy, and Lady Susan hailed her with the request that Miss Portney follow her and led the way into a small thicket, secluded from the passing riders. She brought her horse to a stand.

"Miss Portney, I fear I must ask a favour of you," she said.

Amethy was at once all concern.

A very proper young lady, her hostess thought. "I fear the weather and the chill have allied to make my poor joints the centre of much discomfort. And good Astor's gait is torture for my old bones. Would you trade horses with me?"

Lady Susan could see the confusion and doubt in the young lady's face. Still, the elderly woman held her ground and offered no other explanation. Manners made it imperative that Amethy acquiesce.

"Well...uh...certainly, Lady Susan," Amethy answered. "Starlight, although quite an amenable animal, is not reputed for her gentle gait. But if you feel the change would make the hunt more comfortable—"

"Oh, I certainly do," Lady Susan reiterated. With that she dropped to the ground and with all the appearance of taking the change for granted, unstrapped from the back of her saddle the cloak that she had brought with her.

Amethy reluctantly followed suit.

They were just exchanging the reins when Lady Susan's eye appeared to fall on the lightweight cloak Amethy was holding over her arm.

"My dear, that garment..." Lady Susan said doubtfully, letting her words hang.

Amethy looked down at the cloak and up with some alarm. "Is there something wrong with it?"

"Oh no, it's quite a proper garment," Lady Susan hastened to assure her. "Unfortunately it appears that rain is imminent, and I fear you will be chilled to the bone before you return to Lowestroft."

Amethy nodded. "Possibly I was overly optimistic about the weather," she said. "But there is no hope for it. I would not be so poor of spirit as to leave the hunt just on the chance of inclement weather."

"Ah, but I have the solution," Lady Susan said. "You are in lightweight clothing and carry a lightweight cape. My riding habit and the cloak I brought with me are both too heavy. The answer is quite obvious. Allow me your lighter garment, and my heavier one should suffice to protect you."

While Amethy stared at her wide-eyed, Lady Susan removed from the young lady's unresisting arm the dark blue hooded cape and in its place left the heavier grey wool.

Lady Susan turned a judicious eye to the dark clouds rolling in above. "This is the perfect opportunity to don them. The rain will most certainly fall at any moment."

With that she clasped the cape around her shoulders and raised the hood, urging Amethy to do the same.

"Do pull up the hood," Lady Susan admonished the young lady. "Then you will be prepared."

She reached over and helped Amethy, seeing to it that her face was well protected. She could not think it wonderful that Miss Portney should still be eyeing her with some confusion and speculation. But Lady Susan, intent on her purpose, was not one wit abashed. Once they had remounted, Lady Susan rode off among the few trees and attendant shrubbery to open field beyond.

As she prophesied, she had ridden on the trail of the hunt not more than a quarter of a mile when the rain indeed pelted down. Nor had she gone a mile farther when ahead of her she saw Lord Battenton, his horse impatiently moving under him as he looked back down the field.

Then espying the lady in the blue cloak, riding the pale grey horse, he turned towards her. "Miss Portney," he said. "I fear you are in need of shelter from this downpour. I sent out my carriage in the event of inclement weather. I felt you ladies might prefer to leave the hunt if the storm broke."

Lady Susan, the hood drawn well over her face with the rain as the perfect excuse, nodded and feigned a small sneeze as a reason for not speaking.

"If you would allow me, I will lead you to the carriage and shelter," he persisted.

Again Lady Susan nodded, allowing him to take the reins of the horse and lead her forward. She held the hood down as though protecting herself from the rain.

The downpour had worsened by the time they reached the coach, and Lord Battenton, too, was having some difficulty in protecting his face and his vision. The dispatch with which he handed her into the coach left no opportunity for him to get a look at her face.

Moments later Lady Susan pushed back the hood as the coach rolled away down the road. She removed the cloak, glad that her garments had been protected from the weather. No discomfort must take away the pleasure of seeing Lord Battenton's face if he actually were the one to catch up with the coach first. There were, after all, several gallant gentlemen in the house party, and one in particular needed some new glories to dwell upon—nor would it hurt to bring him out of his comfortable lethargy.

AMETHY, AFTER HAVING BEEN stopped by Lady Susan, was anxious lest she would lose the trail of the hunt and thereby miss Lord Edgemere. The downpour, worsening every minute, made vision difficult, and she was despairing of locating the young man at all when she heard his voice.

Fortunate, she thought, that she recognized it in the rain, for he had not espied her, but was calling out to Lady Susan. Then Amethy realized that riding the large black animal well-known to be the hostess of Lowestroft's mount had caused him to mistake her for that lady.

She slowed and approached him, making herself known.

"Miss Portney," he chattered with relief. "I confess I feared you had been unhorsed and was despairing of locating you."

"Was your concern for me or for my chaperonage of Miss Oglethorpe?" she snapped, her mood lowered by the rain, the effort of controlling the spirited horse and her fatigue from the hunt. But when she saw the young gentleman's confusion and embarrassment, Amethy waved it away. "Pay no attention to me. I will be in a better humour when I am settled within the coach and we are on our way," she said. "The fear that something would prevent us from carrying out our plans has kept me on edge all day."

"This way," he said, and led her cross-country to the road where they found the coach waiting, the coachman slowly walking the horses so they would take no harm from the growing chill.

"I'll ride for a bit and lead your horse," Lord Edgemere said. One look had assured him Miss Oglethorpe and Carrie were indeed inside, and for some odd reason, so was the luggage.

Lord Edgemere's plan was thwarted by Astor, who refused to be led by a stranger. He reared, causing the gentleman to lose his grip on the reins and once free, bolted across the fields.

"He will know his way home," Amethy assured Lord Edgemere.

She stepped into the coach, glad to be out of the weather. Carrie pushed a portmanteau aside to make room for her feet. Before Amethy could remove the soaked cloak, the carriage was rolling along at a good speed. She gazed at her companions.

Miss Oglethorpe was indeed in a state of severe agitation, pale, and wringing a lace handkerchief that was already in shreds. Carrie's grim expression had eased considerably when Amethy entered the coach, but her mouth was still in a straight slash of disapproval.

"Carrie," Amethy admonished her maid. "I declare your attitude will so discomfit me that I will end up following the coach on foot in the rain."

"I cannot think what Lady Halstead will say about this escapade," Carrie returned, not at all admonished by her mistress's disapproval.

Amethy shook out her curls, which had been crushed by the weight of the heavy woollen hood. "She'll be upset at first," Amethy said. "But my aunt is of a decidedly romantic nature. Once she considers the plight of Miss Oglethorpe and Lord Edgemere, she will be quite thrilled by the elopement. By the time we return to Halstead Manor, she will be all agog to hear the circumstances and persuaded we have done exactly as we should."

"I am not convinced of that!" Carrie retorted, but her expression softened.

"You did leave the notes?" Amethy asked. She had spent considerable time the day before committing to paper her apologies to Ladies Halstead and Susan, and knew that Ruth had troubled herself and made many attempts before completing a note to Lord and Lady Battenton.

Even Lord Edgemere had put his pen to paper explaining to General Duckworth as much as he could commit to paper. Those messages were left on the dressing table in Amethy's room where they would be found, but not as quickly as if Lord Edgemere had placed his in his room or Miss Oglethorpe had done the same.

"They were all left," Carrie said, nodding firmly.

"Then we have nothing to worry about." Amethy leaned back to relax. "Before they have knowledge of our intentions and can catch up with us, the deed will be done."

"GAR! BUT YOU'RE a prime bit of flesh and bone," Holmes said, patting the straining shoulders of the hunter he rode.

He was sensible of being upon the back of a blooded animal whose cost he could hardly fathom, but convinced, too, that Lord Northford would value Miss Amethy Portney far beyond an animal, he was not sparing the horse. Still he had come upon no one he could tell of the young lady's plight and was growing desperate.

Then, off to his left he espied General Duckworth who was just riding across the field, leading a large black horse. The animal belonged to Lady Susan. What good it would do to tell General Duckworth of the danger Miss Portney was in, he had no idea, but that was his instruction from Perkins and he turned in the general's direction.

"I say there," the general hailed him the moment he espied the stableman. "Groom at Lowestroft, aren't you?" the old man asked with no preamble.

Holmes nodded, accepting the rise in his station.

"Give a hand in looking for Lady Susan," the general ordered. "Hard to believe she's been unhorsed. Tell you frankly, man, I'm worried about foul play."

Holmes tried to hold the restive hunter still while he shook his head. "Sorry, governor," he said. "But I got me orders and I daren't do but what I'm told. There's plans afoot to kidnap the gentry-mort, Miss Portney, and I'm to warn you and several others so you can protect her."

The general ignored the downpour as he stared at the stableboy. "Knew there was foul play!" he shouted, and pointed to the back of the saddle, where the loose straps showed something had been tied. "She'd of been wearing her cape with the hood up. Think the miscreants could have been bosky and got the wrong woman?"

Holmes was about to disagree, but any excuse to get General Duckworth on the trail of Miss Amethy Portney was good enough. His five years at Lowe-stroft had been enough to assure him that had Lady Susan indeed taken a tumble, the odd affection in which she stood with the neighbourhood assured her of speedy assistance. She was probably already en-sconced by the fire in a neighbouring farmhouse.

Moreover, her huge black hunter, an animal with its own mind, was likely to break away from any stranger as it was trying now to do with General Duckworth. Determined to get aid for Miss Portney in any way he could, Holmes nodded judiciously.

"Think they could have been just cork-brained enough," Holmes announced.

That was enough for the general. He freed the big black horse, rose in the saddle and turned his own mount towards the road. "Follow me, my man! We'll save the lady! Charge!"

As he dashed off Holmes sat on the big hunter for a moment staring after him. "That's a lively old cove,'' he said to himself, and giving the big horse the signal to move, he lunged after the general.

THE EARL OF NORTHFORD CURSED the rain as his big bay hunter cleared a fence but nearly lost his footing on the slick ground. He was considering pulling out of the hunt. The day was advanced, they were not going to catch the fox, and why expose the magnificent animal beneath him to the dangers of a broken leg?

He was suddenly hailed from behind. Turning, he stared. Was Perkins riding one of his blooded animals in the hunt? No. If Perkins found it expedient to bring out one of his employer's hunters in order to catch up with him, something was definitely wrong. Northford drew rein and waited for the groom to catch up with him.

Perkins was breathless from his ride, but the news he brought and all its implications fell on Northford immediately.

"Stick with me," was all he said as he turned Thunder towards the road.

Lord Battenton was capable of pulling such a trick and if Amethy was presented with some logical excuse for travelling in Lord Battenton's company she would do so without hesitation. His warnings to her had fallen on deaf ears. When the young lady said she had never been approached by Lord Battenton, he knew she had never seen his efforts in their true light.

That damned chit had given him more trouble than any woman in his life and was altogether the most interesting female believable. He had tried to push away Jackie's suggestion that she would make a wonderful mother, but despite himself, the idea had rooted itself in his mind and would not give him peace. He'd struggled with it for days; now he found himself enraged that Lord Battenton would dare lay a hand on the young woman who was fast becoming indispensable to his happiness. He was overfilled with a desire for revenge and a need to rescue Amethy.

The early autumn darkness had already fallen, but he was still racing along the road with Perkins in close pursuit when ahead he spotted the lamps of the carriage. The rain had ceased sometime before, but the vehicle was moving at a circumspect speed because of the wet and muddied road.

Northford lunged forward and brought the vehicle to a halt by the simple expedient of catching the lead horse and drawing it up.

"See here," the coachman demanded, and was about to pull a blunderbuss when Perkins rode up beside him and jerked the weapon from his hands.

"Perkins?" The coachman gasped as he recognized the groom from his stay at Lowestroft.

"Hold up there!" Perkins said, and to the surprise of Northford and the coachman, he pulled from his belt a pistol and kept the coachman under surveillance.

Northford jumped from his horse and strode to the door of the carriage just as it opened. When the head and shoulders of a gentleman in riding habit came into view, he grabbed the man by the arm and jerked him from the carriage. His fist was drawn back to deliver the first blow of his rage, when he stopped, his eyes widening.

"Good God, Edgemere?" he exploded. His surprise was heightened by the shrinking belligerence of the young viscount who was bravely squaring away for a regular turn-up. Clearly Lord Edgemere had no ex-

pectation of milling down his opponent, but Northford found himself shying away from a twitching
imitation of the great Belcher's fighting stance.

If that wasn't enough to upset the earl's composure, Miss Portney peered out the carriage door and
her attitude was not that of a young lady being rescued from a fate worse than death.

"Sir! I demand to know the meaning of this!"

Now Northford was even more confused. "Why are
you running away with Edgemere?" he asked, disbe-
lieving.

"I, sir, am not running away with anyone," Amethy retorted. "I insist you unhand this gentleman and
while you're at it, would you please help him put this
luggage in the boot? Miss Oglethorpe and I have no
room to put our feet."

A slow dawning of understanding came over
Northford. Between his relief and the humour of the
situation, he was silent for a moment and then threw
back his head and laughed.

"Under the circumstances I can understand this
precipitous departure from Lowestroft. Miss Portney, I can understand your role, you're the chaperone. What I cannot fathom is why the four of you—"
for he had now looked in the carriage and espied Carrie as well as Miss Oglethorpe "—would crowd your-
selves into the carriage with all your luggage."

"Because that part of the plan went awry," Lord
Edgemere chattered rapidly, his voice after his fright
that of a very young man indeed. "There was no opportunity to get the luggage to the carriage in ad-
vance, and on the road Miss Oglethorpe was too
nervous to wait while it was stored, so it was simply

put up front. The rain has prevented us from stopping to store it properly.''

"Good God," Northford said shaking his head. "Were I eloping, I would do it in a little more comfort. Tell me—what happened to Battenton?''

That remark sufficed to bring puzzled looks from the four who had been riding in the carriage.

"Battenton?" Lord Edgemere asked.

"Lord, man, you don't think I was after you?" Northford answered him. "We'd become privy to a plan that he was kidnapping Miss Portney.''

"I do not understand this constant maligning of Lord Battenton's character on my behalf," Amethy spoke up. "To my knowledge the gentleman never was a threat to me. And besides, it would have been very difficult for him to have located me since Lady Susan exchanged horses—and capes . . .'' Her eyes widened.

Five mouths dropped open as a new and astonishing possibility struck the party on the road. Before they were able to voice their wonder, a pounding of hooves brought the arrival of General Duckworth with Holmes immediately following.

"Good, man, you've got Lady Susan," General Duckworth announced.

"Sorry. Wrong carriage, try on up the road," Northford said with amazing aplomb since they had just ascertained the new situation.

General Duckworth, his military career giving him the experience of making instant decisions, spoke not another word to Northford but turned and looked over his shoulder at Holmes.

"Forward, trooper, we'll save my lady," he said, and dashed off, followed by the undergroom on the big hunter.

Northford watched them as they rode past and then turned to Perkins. "With the quality of ladies at Lowestroft, I can understand this urge for marriage, but why all at one time—and for God's sake, why on my hunters?"

"Oh, they're getting married! I want to go where they're getting married, and I want to get out of this dark place."

This new voice gave everyone pause, for while Miss Oglethorpe, Lord Edgemere and Carrie might not be too familiar with it, Lord Northford, Amethy and Perkins immediately recognized the voice of the little duke. Realizing it came from the back of the carriage, Northford strode around and, with Edgemere's help, unfastened the straps of the luggage flap.

"I don't like riding back here," Jackie said as if it were quite natural to carry on a conversation while sitting in the boot of a coach. "I want to ride up front with you and Miss Amethy when you go to get married. When you get married, can I call her Mama?" He stood up and held out his arms for Lord Northford to help him down.

The earl, so bemused by the sudden appearance of his ward, held him in his arms and stared into his face.

"What on earth?" Amethy gasped. She had stepped out of the carriage, and she walked around to the rear to stand staring at the three boys. "How did they get here?"

"Oh, we were going to save you from that bad man," Willy said. "Only we forgot to bring the magic sword."

"And we didn't bring any sugar biscuits, either," Jackie added. "Am I going to have a mama?" He rubbed the velvet collar on the earl's riding coat as he looked hopefully at his guardian.

"Well...uh...hold it, brat. Not too much along that line has been decided yet," Northford said slowly.

The little duke looked at him with wide eyes. "But you said everybody was getting married."

"Umm...well not... See here, brat, lets just say—"

Northford's discomfited gaze moved between Jackie and Amethy who had suddenly become demure and was staring down at the mud of the road.

"Another pair of shoes ruined," she muttered, unable to remain silent and wanting desperately to change the conversation.

But Northford took a deep breath. "Miss Portney," he said, "you once remarked that Lady Northford would spend a considerable amount of her time refurbishing her wardrobe after the escapades this brat and I would lead her into. Uh...umm...ah, Miss Portney—do you enjoy shopping?"

If Amethy had any doubts that this most confused conversation was a proposal, she was at once convinced of it by the sudden withdrawing of Lord Edgemere and Perkins, each taking one of the Halstead boys with him. That left Amethy, the earl and Jackie, whom the earl was still holding in his arms, at the back of the carriage.

Unable to look him in the eye, she stared down again at her boots. "I confess, my lord, when I am not trapped under fallen roofs, picking myself up out of the ditch or hunting dragons in a cavern, shopping is one of those things I most like to do."

One small, most noble duke, found himself unceremoniously dumped back into the luggage compartment as Northford freed his arms so that he might embrace the young lady.

"I fear you'll have a reputation of being a sad romp. I cannot conceive a day when you will not change before tea from another ruined garment," he said as he drew her to him.

"But we can have lots of sugar biscuits," Jackie said, adding his bit of inducement.

"Sugar biscuits and shopping," Amethy said as she looked up with glowing eyes into Northford's face. "What could be more wonderful?"

"And remember, I did come to rescue a damsel," the earl prompted.

"My own St. George...maybe we'll even find a dragon in the dungeon," Amethy said, smiling up at him.

He gently kissed her lips and would have carried his affections further but a crow of delight from Jackie caused the two lovers to draw apart self-consciously. Again Northford gathered the child in his arms, and the three of them walked around to stand beside the door of the carriage.

Edgemere and Perkins had placed the Halstead boys inside, where they took up all the available room. The floor was filled with luggage, and the ladies were sitting with their feet propped on it. To the crowd in the carriage, Northford added his ward. Then he turned to Edgemere.

"I do believe," he said tranquilly, "that you are starting a new fashion in elopement."

Edgemere grinned. "I was desirous of having chaperonage for Miss Oglethorpe, but I confess, an extra lady, a maid, a gentleman and three children—" and his eyes drifted to Perkins "—and a groom, is a little more than I bargained for." With a gentleman's insight, he added, "I take it you will be going with us to London?"

Northford nodded, then pointed ahead where the lights of a slow-moving carriage were coming down the road. "I think we can dispossess ourselves of a few members," Northford said, reaching in the carriage again to take his ward in his arms. "We'll send the brats and the groom back to Lowestroft. Your company will only be increased by one. It seems I must speak with a certain gentleman whom, if my understanding is correct, is at the present in London on business?" His inquiring look from Amethy brought forth a shy nod. She understood he was speaking of her father.

Perkins hailed the carriage for which General Duckworth and Holmes were now acting as outriders. He, Northford, and Edgemere transferred the children to the carriage returning to Lowestroft.

A small pair of arms tightened their hold around Northford's neck as the earl placed Jackie in the carriage.

"When you come back, will I have a mama?" he asked, suddenly doubtful of his expected happiness.

"I'll do my best, brat," Northford agreed, like the child ignoring the fact that the term would be in spirit and not in fact. "And a whole tin of sugar biscuits."

Amethy walked around the Edgemere carriage, waved and blew a kiss to the boys as Lord Battenton's carriage, with General Duckworth, Holmes and Perkins as escort, started back for Lowestroft Castle.

Jackie, sitting in the carriage beside Lady Susan, waved back and then told Edward and Willy brightly, "I'm going to have sugar biscuits and a mother, too."

Edward leaned forward to look back at the other carriage. He shook his head.

"But we forgot to tell them to bring uth a magic thword," he lisped.

"FOR MY PART, I think it fortunate that Lord Battenton did attempt to kidnap her." Nurse Rae saw the shocked looks on the faces of Tilbin, Perkins and Mrs. Formsby and hastened to explain. "I have no doubt being rescued by Lord Northford overrode her distaste for all those disasters—otherwise she might now be on her way to London alone."

The four original participants of the plot were gathered in the old ballroom again, gathered close to a roaring fire.

Carlyle was above stairs, packing for Lord Northford's stay in London, and Holmes was in the stable, harnessing a team to a carriage, and the two would soon follow the earl.

The other participants had been told briefly of their success in playing Cupid, but the full, scandalous details would only be known by the privileged four now gathered.

"It's settled, right enough," Perkins said, grinning. "And I can tell you, there was no *distaste*—" he emphasized the cramp word "—from either of them."

"Apparently Lord Battenton doesn't know yet," Tilbin informed them.

"He's not returned yet, most likely out chasing a carriage that's already back here," Perkins said. "There'll be a regular dust-up when he finds out...." Perkins looked dissatisfied. "I'd have given a groat to have seen him catch up with that carriage and find Lady Susan in it."

"I declare, such a rescuing of ladies," Mrs. Formsby declared, shaking her head in disbelief. "We might be living in the pages of a book. And to think, Lady Susan is to marry—at her age, too!"

"I dislike having my little gentleman involved," Nurse Rae said. "It seems he's taken no hurt from riding in the back of the coach, but too much excitement cannot be good for him."

"I daresay he will live through it," Tilbin assured her, smiling. "Though I don't think it is over for him. Sammy tells me his Grace overheard a remark made about a wedding trip, and he's already planning on joining his cousin and Miss Portney on theirs."

Nurse Rae bristled. "That I will not countenance. He's been having his way far too often of late. It's unsettling for a child his age."

"Care to wager you won't be packing your trunks?" Perkins asked, smiling. "I'd stake a goodly sum on his wrapping the two of them around his finger."

"Be that as it may, I look forward to seeing Lowestroft full of visitors, with parties and balls," Mrs. Formsby said, smiling. "It will be like old times again."

"If so, I hope the new Lady Northford is not long in taking up residence," Tilbin said. "Lady Susan is much too absentminded to arrange such things."

"You can manage," Perkins said as he stretched his feet to the fire and gave the gathering a mischievous smile. "Have another winter picnic."

For the millions who can't read
Give the Gift of Literacy

One out of five adults in North America
cannot read or write well enough
to fill out a job application
or understand the directions on a bottle of medicine.

**You can change all this by joining the fight
against illiteracy.**

For more information write to:
Contact, Box 81826, Lincoln, Neb. 68501
In the United States, call toll free: 800-228-3225

**The only degree you need
is a degree of caring**

Harlequin
American Romance™
Harlequin celebrates the
American woman...

...by offering you romance stories written
about American women, by American women
for American women. This series offers you
contemporary romances uniquely North American
in flavor and appeal.

◆

Harlequin Temptation™
Passionate stories for
today's woman

An exciting series of sensual, mature stories of
love...dilemmas, choices, resolutions...
all contemporary issues dealt with in a true-to-life
fashion by some of your favorite authors.

◆

Harlequin Intrigue™
Because romance can be quite
an adventure

Harlequin Intrigue, an innovative series that
blends the romance you expect...
with the unexpected. Each story has an added
element of intrigue that provides a new twist to
the Harlequin tradition of romance excellence.

Harlequin Books·

PROD-A-2

Janet Dailey

Dailey

Americana

A romantic tour of America with
Janet Dailey!

Enjoy two releases each month from this
collection of your favorite previously
published Janet Dailey titles, presented
alphabetically state by state.

**Available NOW wherever paperback books
are sold.**